CAPTIVATED BY THE MILLIONAIRE

CAPTIVATED BY THE MILLIONAIRE

NINA SINGH

MILLS & BOON

First published in Great Britain 2019
by Mills & Boon, an imprint of HarperCollins*Publishers*
1 London Bridge Street, London, SE1 9GF

Large Print edition 2019

ISBN: 978-0-263-08256-2

MIX
Paper from
responsible sources
FSC® C007454

This book is produced from independently certified FSC™ paper to ensure responsible forest management. For more information visit www.harpercollins.co.uk/green.

Printed and bound in Great Britain
by CPI Group (UK) Ltd, Croydon, CR0 4YY

To the Mills & Boon editors
I've had the fortune to work with—
Flo Nicoll, Vic Britton and Laurie
Johnson. For all your guidance,
encouragement and just
overall fabulousness, I feel
truly blessed as an author.

PROLOGUE

HE'D ALWAYS PRIDED himself on being prepared. Overly prepared, in fact. But damned if he'd seen any of this coming.

Jordan Paydan stood in front of the glass wall of his Upper East Side Manhattan penthouse and stared at the paperwork that had just been delivered to him via special messenger. No detail had been left up to chance. Every "i" had been dotted; every "t" had been crossed. A slew of family practice attorneys had made sure to look over each piece of paper.

And now Jordan's life would never be the same.

His stepmother hadn't put up any kind of a fight; she'd simply waited for the funds to be transferred into her account. He grunted a laugh at the term. *Stepmother.* The woman was barely older than his own thirty-one years. She certainly didn't appear to want to act like a responsible adult. He didn't know her well at all, but that much about her was as clear as the sky on this bright New York afternoon. Considering the events of the past few months and based on the paperwork he currently held in his hands, his stepmother had no qualms about moving on after his father's death.

Jordan uttered a small curse and threw the envelope and documents onto the mahogany desk behind him next to the couch.

Nothing to do now but to try and plan for the colossal changes that were about to overtake his very existence. None of which were his own doing in any way. He just had to figure out where exactly to start.

CHAPTER ONE

Six months later

JESSALYN RAFFI WAS completely engrossed in the mural she was painting on the wall. It was good. Really good, if she did say so herself. She'd spent most of the day painstakingly drawing and creating a detailed image of a majestic, ancient castle sitting atop a grand mountain. Fat, fluffy clouds floated above its towers. She'd even thrown in a few knights on steeds along its base.

Jess had no doubt the child about to occupy this room as a new resident of this house was going to love it. What child wouldn't? To be able to walk into your bedroom and feel like you could be transported through time and space into an entirely different reality would seem magical to any youngster. She was certain of it.

As engrossed as she was, she didn't even hear

the front door open and close downstairs; nor did she hear the steady sound of footsteps as someone came up the stairs and approached the open door. It took her a moment to realize that someone now stood right outside in the hallway. So it was no wonder she shrieked as loud as she did when she finally understood she was no longer alone. A strange man stood staring at her. Out of sheer reflex, she threw the wet paintbrush she held directly at his chest like some sort of futile weapon, her aim finding its target straight and center.

"What the hell?" a deep masculine voice responded with outrage.

She realized her mistake almost immediately. But it was too late. An angry splotch of red paint spread and splattered across the newcomer's shirt.

His clearly expensive, well-tailored silk shirt.

He was no intruder. In fact, if she had to hedge a bet, Jess would guess he was the new homeowner. And she'd attacked him with a messy wet paintbrush.

She rushed over immediately, grabbing her damp rag off the floor along the way. "Oh, my

God. I'm so sorry. It's just that you startled me." But her attempts to try and wipe the paint off his chest only served to make matters worse. The splotchy stain simply spread across the fabric of his shirt into one big blob of bright red. The more she tried to mop it up, the messier things got.

"Please stop," he commanded through gritted teeth, his hands clenched at his sides. No doubt he was willing himself to keep from forcefully grabbing her hands and pushing her away. To his credit, he didn't.

Jess wanted to sink into the floor. "I'm so sorry," she repeated. "What in the world are you doing here?"

He blinked at her, anger clouding his eyes. "This is my house. I should be the one asking you that question."

Through her mortification, Jess finally allowed herself to look at the man's face. Lordy, he was so utterly striking. Sandy-blond hair just dark enough that he couldn't be described as fair. Just enough facial hair that added a rugged masculinity to his face. Piercing grayish-green eyes. He stood about a head taller than she did.

Even in his annoyed state, it was impossible not to notice just how handsome he was.

"But I had no idea you were due to arrive," she stammered through her embarrassment. "Marie told me you wouldn't be here until tomorrow morning. She owns the contracting company you hired. Just so happens she's a friend of mine. Throws me odd jobs here and there." Now she was just blabbering. *Get a grip.* She took a deep breath before continuing. "I was just finishing up." She pointed to the massive painting on the wall behind her.

He didn't even glance at it. "None of that explains why you're here at this hour. Nor why my front door was unlocked."

She shrugged, tried to smile. It didn't quite manifest. "I guess I lost track of time. Like I said, I was working on the mural."

A momentary pause of silence ensued in which he simply stood and studied her. Jess turned away when she couldn't stand the scrutiny any longer. "It's a castle," she unnecessarily informed him.

"Why?"

She turned back to face him as the single word hung in the air. "Why? Why what?"

He let out a long, clearly frustrated breath. "Why are you painting a mural in the first place? I asked my assistant to hire contractors simply to apply fresh paint through the house. They were given very specific instructions regarding color scheme. Instructions that I was told were relayed to the painters."

Jess cleared her throat, trying not to get flustered. She had to keep her cool here. "Yes, I know. Eggshell white. Throughout the whole house." How did he not see how utterly bland and boring that was? Eggshell white could hardly be considered a *color scheme* for heaven's sake. She kept that thought to herself.

He gave one sharp nod. "Correct. Very simple. At no point was there any request for a medieval castle complete with towers and banners to be drawn on the wall."

A lump had formed in her throat. "I realize that. But I was told this was to be the child's room and I thought any little boy or girl would appreciate—"

He cut her off with a dismissive wave of his

hand. “Regardless of what you thought, you took it upon yourself to do something that resulted in a delay to my schedule.”

She tried not to cringe. He sort of had a point about that. “I apologize. But it will only take me a few more minutes to finish up.”

He squinted at her, eyebrows drawn over tight, dark, piercing eyes. “The little girl who is to occupy this room is due to arrive in just a few minutes with her little pink pony air mattress ready to inflate. Thanks to you, she won’t be able to spend the first night in her new home in her new room.”

Okay. Another good point. But it wasn’t as if there was a shortage of rooms in the house. The place was a downright mansion for heaven’s sake. Another point she wasn’t going to bring up. “Again, I apologize,” she simply repeated. “I’ll just finish up really quickly.”

But he wasn’t listening. In fact, he had stepped aside and was motioning toward the stairs. “Please just leave.”

Jess swallowed past the lump that had now grown to brick size. Damn it. She wasn’t going to tear up and cry. Not in front of this cranky, rude stranger. She’d only been trying to do something nice for a small child. Without a word, she swiftly began to gather her things.

Like the saying went, no good deed and all that.

Jordan watched the young lady descend the stairs and make a beeline to the door. He thought for sure she'd slam it behind her but surprisingly, she didn't. Just shut it slowly with a soft click of the handle. But there was no doubt she was in a hurry to get out of the house. Well, who could blame her? After the way he'd behaved just now, it was no wonder she wanted out. He'd almost called her back to apologize as she rushed down the stairs. Perhaps he should have. But it had been such a long day and all he'd wanted to do was check out the new house then take a long shower. Only to find a strange woman hovering about. He rubbed a hand down his face and grabbed his hastily packed overnight bag from the hallway where he'd thrown it. He'd just driven four straight hours, some of it through pouring rain, on the speakerphone for most of the time, dealing with a major proposal with an important investor. He could hardly be blamed for being a little short after finding an unexpected woman in his home upon arrival. Not to mention she'd ruined one of his good shirts. No, he couldn't really be faulted for the way he'd reacted.

Could he?

Jordan gave a shake of his head. What was done was done. He couldn't take it back now. There was nothing for it. What was he supposed to do? Find out exactly who she was from the contracting company then try to contact her to apologize? He didn't have that kind of spare time. And trying to catch up to her now was just downright silly. So why was he entertaining the notion of doing just that? He had to shake off the useless thoughts.

And anyway, Elise was due to arrive with little Sonya in a few minutes and he'd be too busy getting everyone set up for the night in the new place. He barely had time for a shower at this point.

Despite the press of time, Jordan turned to the painted wall of the mural she'd been working on. Now that he was truly looking at it, he had to admit what a work of art it was. Walking over, he studied the painting further, for that was what it truly was—an artistic painting. Full of detail and color, down to the tiny knights on horseback climbing the side of the mountain. She'd done all this freehand. The level of detail was breathtaking. And he'd chastised her for it.

Perhaps an attempt to find her and apologize wasn't such a far-fetched idea after all.

Despite the overwhelming paint smell, he'd gotten a small whiff of her subtle lilac scent when she'd brushed by him as she left the room. He couldn't remember the last time he'd noticed a woman's scent. He recalled the uncomfortable silence and tension in the air as she'd gathered her things, biting her bottom lip no doubt to try and hide the trembling. That thought had his shame growing.

There was no denying he'd behaved like a complete bastard. No excuse would change that fact. Yet more proof that he didn't have the temperament or the patience to be the sole guardian of a little girl. But he'd had no choice, had he?

His father's words echoed through his mind. *You have to take her, Jordan. Her mother doesn't want her. I know how much I'm asking of you.*

Well, Martha's Vineyard was a small island, the major reason they were moving here. The sort of place where everyone frequented the same establishments. Chances were probably quite high that he'd run into the artist again at some point. When he did, he'd be sure to make a genuine and heartfelt apology.

No use beating himself up about it right now.

By the time he dried off, Jordan had convinced himself even further that he'd be able to make amends. He was bound to run into the young lady one way or another. Not only would he apologize, he would also make sure to compliment her on her clear artistic talent. Maybe he'd even get a chance to explain that he dealt with curt, cutthroat business people every day in his professional life. Sometimes, that curtness spilled over into his own behavior, particularly on days like the one today had been.

The notion of being able to explain himself served to bolster his mood. And it absolutely had nothing to do with the prospect of running into the artistic painter at some point in the future.

He heard the front door open downstairs followed by Elise's feminine voice announcing their arrival. After throwing on a pair of sweats and soft cotton T-shirt, he made his way downstairs.

"You found the place okay, then?" he asked the nanny, who was in the process of helping Sonya out of her bright pink hoodie.

"Yep."

"Hey, sport," he said as he tousled the little girl's hair. She responded with a simple wave and a small, shy smile. Not that he'd expected it, but a part of him still reeled at the lack of a verbal response. Since slowly and gradually losing her ability to hear, the child had become less and less willing to speak. It was tearing him up inside, despite what all the experts said about such a response being common and expected.

He leaned down to her height and signed that he was happy to see her. That earned him a toothless grin. They were both just recently starting to get the hang of using sign language. Though barely six, Sonya was a quick and motivated learner. In fact, she was picking up on the skill faster than he was.

"She looks tired." He stood, addressing Elise.

"And hungry. It was a long ride. Though Sonya did enjoy the ferry from the Cape."

"I saw a pizza place not too far away on my ride over. Hope they deliver."

"If they don't, I call 'not it' on driving to pick it up. I've had enough traveling."

"Fine," he relented. "Then after that we'll get her settled and into bed," he said out loud but made a cupped hand sleeping motion to Sonya. She nodded in response.

"She's excited to see her new room," Elise said. "Can I take her up for a quick look before dinner?"

"There's a surprise waiting for her there."

Elise raised an eyebrow with curiosity. Jordan held his hand out to Sonya. "Let's go see," he told her, not sure how much she would hear him but knowing she'd understand.

Once they got there, Sonya's eyes grew wide. She clapped in pure joy when she saw the castle painted on the wall. Another pang of guilt slammed through Jordan's chest. The beautiful painter had been right all along. Sonya was delighted with the image. She ran over to the wall to take a closer look. Elise had started recording the little girl's reaction with her mobile phone. Sonya paced along the wall, taking in every detail, smiling in delight.

"That's amazing," Elise said behind him. "How thoughtful of you to commission someone to do such a thing, Jordan. Someone obviously very talented."

If she only knew. An image suddenly flashed in his mind—of a dark-haired beauty in paint-splattered overalls trying desperately to control her trembling bottom lip. Sonya ran back to him and hugged his leg in delight. He could only rub the top of her small head.

"Ank oo," she said in a tiny, strained voice.

Jordan cursed under his breath as he bit back the sudden choking feeling at the base of his throat. Sonya's attempt at speaking was such a rare occurrence these days.

Yeah, he owed someone a heck of an apology.

The little girl was ignoring her. Or she was playing a little game of sorts. One thing was for certain; Jess wasn't familiar with the child at all, had never seen her before here at the Vineyard Vine's Children's Center. Or anywhere else on the island, for that matter. The center provided a central location for all sorts of activities and classes, including child care and creative arts for young children, as well as athletic pursuits such as gymnastics and swim lessons in the regulation-size pool behind the building. Jess had been teaching painting there part-time for the better part of three years. And she loved every minute of it. Perhaps she had a new pupil. The girl's mother was probably in the office right behind them signing her up for classes.

Jess realized her mistake as soon as she approached the child. She hadn't been ignoring her at all. The clearly startled expression on her face when Jess reached her side told her she hadn't heard when Jess had said hello from behind her.

She had a hearing impairment.

Jess had enough experience working with small children that she had a rudimentary knowledge of sign language. Crouching down to eye level with her, she signed *hello.*

The child's response was a wide smile and a small wave.

My name is Jess.

The little girl spelled out her name in ASL. *Sonya.*

Hello, Sonya. I'm so happy to meet you.

That earned her another smile.

Jess pointed to the bulletin board the girl had been staring at when she'd come upon her. Specifically, her gaze seemed to be focused on a flyer announcing the summer play. Jess and a couple of other teachers had volunteered to help the children put together an elementary performance of *Mother Goose.*

If the girl was new in town, the play might be a perfect way to get her acclimated to her new community. Jess pointed to the caption on the flyer that read *Parts Still Available*. Then she pointed to Sonya's chest.

"Would you like to be in the play? There are still spots open, and we've only just begun rehearsals. I'm one of the teachers in charge. And we'd love to have you."

Sonya seemed to understand at least the gist of what Jess was asking her. She tapped her finger on the flyer once more. The little girl's eyes widened as she pondered the question.

Her impairment wouldn't be a problem at all, Jess figured. They could certainly adapt a part that would work for her easily enough. At this age, the children were so young, none of them were actually saying many lines anyway.

"What do you think?" Jess asked. "Would you like to be in the play?"

The glass door of the office opened just then and a harsh male voice suddenly boomed behind her. A somewhat familiar voice, at that.

"What in devil's name?"

She turned to find the last person in the world she'd been expecting here. The cranky grouch from the other night. The one who'd yelled at her about her castle.

Hard to believe, but he seemed even more upset with her now than he'd been then.

Jordan's surprise at seeing the young artist again quickly turned to ire when he realized what she was up to. Had she really just asked Sonya to be in some sort of preschool performance? What could she possibly be thinking? To think for a split second, when he'd first seen her out here in this hallway, he'd actually felt grateful at the prospect of being able to apologize for his behavior the other night. As if.

She straightened at his question. "What are you doing here?" she demanded to know, her eyes shooting daggers his way.

Not that it was any of her business, but he

responded to her question, the one she'd asked with scorn and derision clear in her voice. As if she should be the one to be outraged in the current scenario. "I'm signing her up for swimming classes." Jordan wanted to get the errand out of the way first thing after they'd settled in. The L-shaped pool in his new backyard was deep enough to be concerning. Not to mention the Atlantic Ocean a stone's throw away.

He didn't really have time to stand here and answer her questions. The woman was a repetitive thorn in his side and he didn't even know who she was.

It was his turn to demand some answers. "What exactly were you asking her?"

Sonya stood staring at them from one to another. She appeared to be smiling at the exchange.

"First of all, please check your tone. Secondly, I was merely asking Sonya if she wanted to participate in the preschool play. Hardly an unforgivable offense."

"She doesn't. She's not interested."

Her eyes narrowed on him and she crossed her arms in front of her chest. "Shouldn't she have any kind of say in the matter?"

"She's barely six. Why would you even ask her to make such a decision?"

"Because I teach a class here and also volunteer to put together the annual summer play." She extended her hand. "I'm Jess. Jessalyn Raffi."

Jordan shook the hand she offered and introduced himself, reflexively and out of sheer common courtesy, despite his impatience.

The introductions seemed to somehow only further increase the awkwardness.

She cleared her throat before continuing. "Your daughter seemed interested in the flyer and—"

He cut her off. "Sister."

She blinked. "I beg your pardon?"

"She's not my daughter. She's my sister. And she won't be acting in some play."

"She's your sister?" She sounded incredulous.

"Half sister to be totally accurate." Jordan rammed a hand through his hair in frustration. Again, none of this was any of her business.

"I see," Jess responded. "Why?"

Was she serious? "Why is she my sister?"

She gave a small shake of her head. "No. Why don't you want her to be in the play? I think it would give her a chance to get to know other children. I know you're new to Martha's Vineyard."

If she couldn't guess why, he wasn't going to explain it to her.

Between Sonya's difficulties with her hearing and her reluctance to speak, being involved in a play could open her to all sorts of taunts from the other children.

Damned if he would put Sonya through such exposure and embarrassment.

Not after all that she'd already been through.

CHAPTER TWO

JORDAN WAS FEELING like a heel once more. And Sonya had made it clear she thought he'd acted like one during the entire ride back home from the community center. Perhaps he'd overreacted back there. Again. But something about the woman seemed to be making him act like a curmudgeon whenever he saw her. He couldn't explain it.

It probably had something to do with the way she'd assumed his sister would want a hand-drawn immaculate castle on her bedroom wall. Or that she'd get some sort of social benefit from participating in a community center children's play.

But it turned out she was a teacher. So she probably knew quite a bit about school-age children. More so than he did, certainly. Now he could only watch as Sonya was frantically relaying what had transpired at the center to Elise, using hand gestures and a writing pad.

When she was done, they both turned to give him glaring looks of disapproval.

He threw his hands up in surrender. "Okay, look. I admit I could have handled it better. Especially considering I already chewed her out our first night here."

They both looked at him in shock. "What are you talking about?" Elise demanded to know.

Damn it. He hadn't meant to let that slip. Jordan stared up at the ceiling as he explained. "It just so happens, she's the artist who's responsible for the castle on the wall upstairs."

His little sister's mouth formed a surprised round O. He continued, "Only, I wasn't expecting to see anyone here at that hour when I arrived and I sort of communicated my displeasure about it."

Elise swore in some unknown dialect. She was fluent in three languages and he never knew which one she was speaking when she did that. "And you admonished her again today? Simply because she asked Sonya about participating in a play at the children's center?"

Well, when she put it that way… "Why would Sonya want to be in some silly play?" he asked what he thought was a fairly obvious question under the circumstances.

Elise rammed her hands on her hips as Sonya continued to glare his way.

"Why wouldn't she?" Elise asked.

Were they really going to make him come out and say it?

He could only glance from one small outraged face to the other adult one. Finally, after several tense moments of silence, Elise spared him from having to answer. She tousled Sonya's hair and signed for her to go upstairs to wash up before her afternoon snack.

"Look," she began once the little girl left the room. "I know you're trying to do the right thing, but you can't be so overprotective of her. It's not good for anyone, least of all Sonya."

She was the only one who dared to talk back to him in such a manner. Not even his merciless business colleagues came close. "After what she's been through, how can you blame me?"

"The accident was months ago, Jordan. And the doctors keep telling you it had nothing to do with what she's dealing with in terms of her hearing."

"But it may have triggered it."

"They said that's just a theory. In either case, you've upended your whole life with this move in response."

He shrugged. "I'll do whatever it takes to help her get through this."

"Including letting her grow up like any other little girl?"

"But she's not."

"Oh, Jordan."

This was a useless conversation. He was responsible for Sonya now. Damned if he would allow her to be hurt any more than she already had been. Especially considering her suffering may be in part his fault.

"I have work to do," he told Elise in clear dismissal.

Luckily, she didn't push, just silently turned away and moved toward the kitchen to prepare Sonya's snack. But the rigidity of her back made it clear exactly what she thought of Jordan Paydan at the current moment.

Great. Now he'd gone and made three females upset with him, including two who lived under the same roof. That was going to make for a very long dinner and evening.

As far as Jessalyn Raffi, it appeared now that

a mere verbal apology would no longer suffice given the repeat offense. Good thing he'd noticed a florist shop near the local pizza place. Looked like he'd be giving it some business in the very near future. In fact, he figured it would probably be wise to order three bouquets considering the total number of females currently upset with him.

Jess was running late again. Her summer children's art class she taught would be starting in about half an hour. She wasn't even inside her classroom yet. Given that some of the children always arrived a little early, she needed to get going already.

But her night had been restless and fretful, full of fanciful dreams that had taken her by surprise. Dreams that involved a dark, tall, enigmatic man with grayish, hardened eyes. It made no sense. But she was torn between outrage at his attitude toward her during their meeting and a strange feeling of intrigue.

Uh-oh. Jess didn't dare follow this path again. She'd already had her fair share of experience with an overbearing man who was all too quick to dismiss her opinion.

Still, she couldn't seem to dampen her curiosity. Who was Jordan exactly? Why was he here? Wealthy tourists and seasonal residents flocked to the island every year during these summer months. Everyone from Hollywood megastars to political elites. But not many folks made the vineyard their permanent home. What had made Jordan decide to do so?

And why was he his little sister's guardian?

Though she only taught part-time, Jess had been around enough children to know that families came in all sorts of shapes and sizes. But Jordan and Sonya's particular scenario definitely had her curiosity piqued.

Right. As if she could actually deny the real reason she was so curious. Something about him called to her in a way she couldn't explain.

She pushed open the door to the class building and nearly ran into Clara, the center's director.

"I've been waiting for you to come in!" the older woman declared as Jess fought to retain her balance before dropping all her art supplies. "You've been holding out on us."

"I beg your pardon?"

"Who's the mystery man?" Clara asked.

Had she sent Clara a text or email in her sleep during one of her Jordan dreams? The mere possibility of the absurd thought had her horrified.

"Mystery man?"

"Let's go to your classroom," Clara simply stated without clarifying anything about what she was referring to. She'd definitely walked into some sort of unexpected mystery this morning. One she didn't really have time for, Jess thought, glancing at the industrial wall clock hanging above the door.

It all made sense once they arrived in the classroom she usually taught in. An elaborate display of colorful, exotic flowers adorned the entire surface of the long supply table that sat next to her easel.

"Who are they from?" Clara wanted to know.

Did she dare hope? That was silly. Why would Jordan Paydan send her flowers, and such elaborate ones, no less?

"They must have cost a fortune!" Clara declared.

"I—I don't know."

Clara gave her a disbelieving look. "Well, go on. Take a look at the card, then."

Jess slowly set down her paints and charcoal pencils and walked over to the centerpiece—a tall glass vase with a large elegant red bow at its base. A delightful scent of lilies, orchids and lilacs tickled her nose as she approached. The sender must have bought out half of Bower's Flowers in the center of town. She removed the card and pulled it out of the envelope. Shockingly enough, the flowers *were* from Jordan. Her mouth went dry as she read the tiny font.

Please accept the flowers along with my apologies for my inexcusable behavior.
Jordan Paydan

She read it again, the words slightly blurred now as her hand was shaking for some strange reason. Simple. Direct. But she couldn't help but feel touched. He'd gone out of his way during a no doubt stressful and busy move to take the time to send her flowers. Most men would have simply called or waited for an opportunity to present itself. The man she'd been briefly involved with during college probably wouldn't have even done that much. In fact, she could count on one hand all the times she'd been sent flowers from a man.

Though Jordan had certainly overdone it. A simple bouquet would have sent the same message. A single rose would have, in fact. Jordan was clearly the type who spent an exorbitant amount of money to make a simple apology. An uncomfortable sensation tingled at the base of her spine at that thought.

"Well?" Clara broke into her musings. "Don't keep me in the dark any longer. This is so exciting," she said and clapped her hands in front of her chest.

Clara was in for a disappointment. "It's nothing to be excited about, I'm sorry to say."

Her smile faded. "But these are gorgeous. It's such a romantic gesture."

Jess shook her head. "Hardly. They're simply meant as an apology."

"An apology?"

"That's right."

"From whom?"

"There's a new family on the island. They've just moved in." She paused, trying to find the right words to explain how this all came about. "Our first couple of meetings didn't exactly go well."

"I see."

"I'll have to find a way to tell him all is forgiven," Jess said, glancing at the card once more. "I think he signed the little girl up for a swimming class the other day. We might have their contact information."

"Who is it? I did most of the recent sign-ups myself."

"Jordan Paydan."

A flash of recognition crossed Clara's face. "Jordan? Why didn't you say so?"

"You know him?"

"Most of the locals do. Well, they know of him anyway."

"They do?" Jess had only lived on the vineyard for about three years. Compared to some of the families who had been here for generations and lived here year-round, she was considered a newbie—barely more than a long-term tourist.

Clara explained, "Jordan's mother was born here in town and grew up not too far from the center, in fact. She used to take classes as a little girl. Mostly athletics. Quite the gymnast."

"I had no idea."

"She left as a young lady and made quite a name for herself as a successful fashion model in New York City. Such a shame what happened."

Clara definitely had Jess's full attention now. But she didn't get a chance to ask as several of her pupils entered the room. Class was due to start in about five minutes.

Clara motioned toward the bouquet. "So nothing romantic behind this at all?" she wanted to know as one child waved to them both and took her seat.

"Not even a little."

The disappointment that settled behind Clara's eyes was as clear as the vivid colors of her bouquet. "What a shame. But such a nice gesture on his part."

Jess simply nodded. *Nice*. Yes, that was all it was. Jordan was being apologetic and conciliatory by sending her flowers, as beautiful and expensive as they were. Who knew, perhaps he'd run their encounters by a girlfriend or even a wife who'd admonished him and urged him to apologize.

That possibility sent a tightening sensation in the center of her gut. How silly of her. She'd met the man exactly twice under less than cordial circumstances both times.

But she couldn't deny how intrigued she was by Jordan and whatever his story was. Not many newcomers moved here permanently in general. Though VIPs ranging from politicians to movie stars to famous authors had property throughout the island, not many of them stuck around permanently after the summer months. What had made Jordan come? Why was he taking care of his sister by himself? What had happened to her parents? To his parents? Curiosity about the possible answers dug at her.

More than she cared to admit.

Jordan had to get out of this blasted study and get some air. Or food. Or something. Though his home office was large and expansive, he was starting to feel a bit stifled. This room was a far cry from the Manhattan high-rise office building he used to occupy. He was successful enough as a venture capitalist now that he could do most of his business out of any office he chose with a few trips into the city throughout the month to meet face-to-face with colleagues as the need arose. But moving to a New England coastal island was still going to be quite the adjustment. He'd done it for

Sonya's sake and he was still convinced that getting her out of New York City was the wise choice.

But now he was feeling restless. What was there to do around here in the middle of the day?

A pair of bright hazel eyes and silky brunette hair flashed in his mind. Had she received the flowers yet? He wondered what her reaction had been when they'd arrived. Did she like the arrangement? He couldn't count the number of times he'd sent flowers to women throughout his adult life. Never before had he wondered about their reaction.

Truth be told, he couldn't blame her if she'd taken one look at the card and thrown them out the window. Given the way he'd treated her, it would serve him right. Something told him she wasn't the type to do such a thing. No, she was more the sort who would give them away to a girlfriend if she didn't like the flowers.

He'd just been taken by such surprise when he'd walked over to find her asking Sonya about participating in a play. It had nothing to do with his shock at seeing her again. Right. If he repeated that enough, he might somehow convince himself. Damn it. He didn't seem to know how to act around her. What the hell was his problem? Jordan sighed and stood up abruptly from his desk. His focus was shot; may as well take a walk.

He wasn't terribly shocked at where he found himself several moments later—outside the red-brick building that was home to the community center. He could see her through the first-floor window. Jessalyn Raffi. She'd introduced herself as Jess at first. Jordan watched as she walked around from table to table, assisting various children with their projects. Even from this distance he could see the splatter of paint on her smock and all over her hands. Her hair was done up in a loose, haphazard bun. There was a gypsy-like, bohemian quality about her he couldn't help but find intriguing.

Somehow, she even made a smock look sexy.

Stop it!

He gave his head a shake and turned to walk away. But then she suddenly looked up, right in his direction. Damn it. Now he'd been caught watching her. What must she be thinking? He was so far off his game when it came to this woman, he hardly recognized himself. Well, he wasn't going to turn and walk away. That would look even worse.

He had to do something. A long, shrill bell sounded and the children all suddenly stood up and started picking up their projects. He dared another look at her, bracing for the scorn and derision he'd see on her face. Instead, she smiled at him.

He had to suck in a breath. Jordan made up his mind and started walking toward the entrance before he could give it too much thought.

The last of the children were slowly straggling out to their awaiting parents as he reached her doorway.

He cleared his throat once they were alone. "I was—uh…just out taking a walk." That was the way, fella. Just dazzle her with some witty conversation. He wouldn't be surprised if she rolled her eyes at him.

"I'm glad you did," she responded instead. "It gives me a chance to say thank you." She gestured to the long wooden supply table that housed the flowers. "They're lovely. But it wasn't necessary."

He shrugged. "I'm glad you like them. And

an apology was definitely required after…well, you know."

She sucked in her bottom lip, the small, subconscious gesture sent a strange bolt of heat through his chest. Then she shook her head in disagreement. "No. As far as the first night, you were right. I had no business deciding what to put on your wall. I wanted to tell you I'm sorry."

Now *she* was apologizing to *him* and it made him feel like a complete heel.

She continued, "It was rather forward of me. It's just, sometimes I get inspired and don't think things through."

For someone like him, it was a novel concept. He'd always been one who preferred structure, planned even the most minute details of a project well in advance. So the next words out of his mouth were so surprisingly spontaneous, he could hardly believe he was about to say them.

"Actually, I wanted to talk to you about that."

She ducked her head, as if chagrined. "Of course. I'll be sure to tell Marie that someone needs to head down and paint the eggshell white over the castle. Free of charge, obviously. I'd do it myself but—"

Jordan cut her off with a shake of his head. "That's not what I meant."

Her gaze narrowed on him when she looked back up. "It's not?"

"No. In fact, you mentioned that night that the castle wasn't quite finished. I'd very much like it if you would complete whatever else you meant to add. And this time, you'll be paid for your work. It's only fair."

"Wow, I definitely did not see that coming," she stammered, clearly shocked at his proposal.

The truth was, so was he.

CHAPTER THREE

IF SOMEONE HAD told her forty-eight hours ago that she'd be back in this house at the request of the new owner to finish her painting, Jess would have asked them if they had a bridge they wanted to sell her. But here she was, outlining in charcoal pencil the rest of the scene she'd had in mind when she'd first imagined it in her head.

Jordan was in the mansion somewhere and she felt his presence fully, kept looking over her shoulder to the hallway in case he walked past. So far he hadn't. She had absolutely no reason to feel disappointed by that. It pained her but she had to admit to never before being quite so aware of a man. Not even Gary when she'd first met him. It had taken time for her feelings for her former fiancé to develop. Her only other relationship after Gary could only be described as a summer fling, though she'd been woefully naive in believing it might have led to more. That particular gentleman had simply taken off without so much as a goodbye at the end of the vineyard's tourist season. All the more reason to squash her current attraction to Jordan Paydan with haste.

Jess returned her focus to her artwork. She was simply here to do a job. Once she got lost in a project, the rest of the world would often disappear. She needed that phenomenon to happen right now. Regardless of the fact that a man she felt more aware of than she ever had anyone else happened to be under the same roof.

The sound of footsteps approaching in the hallway broke into her thoughts. She sensed him behind her and her heart did a small leap in her chest.

"So the moat, then. That's what you needed to complete," he said in a smooth, low voice that sent waves of electricity over her skin.

"And the drawbridge," she told him. "That's next."

He walked into the room to stand beside her. A tremble suddenly developed in her hand and she had to force herself to steady it or her lines would be shot. She couldn't even put her finger on why her attraction to him was just so notable, and there was no denying that was what she felt right now—pure, animalistic attraction. But this time was different, much stronger.

And what did that say about her previous long-term relationship? Had she ever actually felt a quake in her center when Gary had walked into the room? If so, she couldn't recall. No, she'd admitted to herself long ago that Gary had simply been a grasp at some sort of stability. After the constant upheavals that defined her childhood, she'd been more than impatient to find a grounded life with some semblance of a routine and a steady anchor. So she'd rushed into a relationship that was doomed to fail.

Studying Jordan now, she realized the two men really couldn't be compared. There really was no comparison. First of all, Jordan had apologized for being rude to her, even if he had done it in a somewhat overblown way by ordering half the flower selection at Bower's Flowers.

Gary had never once uttered the word *sorry*, no matter how much in the wrong he'd been during their arguments. Arguments that had only grown more and more frequent after she'd made her decision to leave grad school.

Not to mention Jordan had been trying to protect his little sister when he'd confronted her. Jess couldn't really take his reaction personally.

"I suppose that makes sense," Jordan said. "You can't have a moat without a drawbridge."

"True."

He stepped closer to examine her work and the scent of him reached her, a subtle woodsy scent that well suited him.

It was settled. She was way too distracted to keep trying to draw. She tucked her pencil above her left ear and turned to face him. He had on an ocean-blue T-shirt that brought out the dark hue of his eyes and fit him just well enough to see a hardened, muscular chest underneath.

"Do you mind my asking what made you change your mind? About the diorama?" she asked. A disquieting thought had been nagging at her about the whole turnaround since he'd asked and she'd accepted the other day.

He shrugged. "It's quite a simple answer, really."

"Which is?"

"You were right. She did like it. Her reaction upon first entering the room was one of pure joy and awe."

The thought of that made her heart tingle in her chest. Yes! That was exactly why she felt such a calling to do such things, for the joy it would bring to others. Particularly when it came to little children.

"I'm so glad to hear that. And a little relieved."

"Relieved?"

She shrugged her shoulders. "I thought maybe you were just trying to make amends. Like with the flowers."

He laughed. "No, the flowers were an apology. This was more of a *mea culpa*. To admit that you were spot-on that day. Sonya did love it when she saw it, exactly as you said. Sonya will be thrilled to see the artwork has been extended."

"She's not here?"

He shook his head. "No, Elise took her out to do some shopping."

Elise. So she'd been right. There was a girlfriend, after all. Maybe she was even more than that. For all she knew, he could actually be married. Hardly surprising given the man in question. Handsome, successful, charming. Men like Jordan weren't often single. Not for long anyway.

Not that it was any of her business.

"In any case," Jordan continued. "Thank you for giving up your Saturday to finish up. I know it has to be an inconvenience."

"It's my pleasure," Jess responded, somewhat disheartened now that she knew another woman would be returning to the house soon. A woman that shared his house and his ward. And most likely, his bed. "I'm glad I got a chance to finish." The best thing to do for her now would be to just finish up and then be on her way. Back to her ordinary, staid life where she had to pretend Jordan Paydan did not exist. She pulled her pencil back out. The sooner she made progress on the painting, the better. Then she could start the process of licking her proverbial wounds.

"You'll have to tell me what Sonya thinks when she sees it," she said as she went back to work.

"I'm sure she'll love it. In fact, she'll be thrilled. She's a very exuberant little girl."

Jess couldn't help but laugh. That was certainly the impression she'd gotten of Sonya during their brief encounter the other day. "It definitely shows just by the sparkle she seems to have in her eyes."

"I'd say that's a perfect way to describe my sister. You're very observant, Ms. Raffi.

"It's why I thought to ask her about being in the school play." Jess wanted to kick herself as soon as the words left her mouth. She wished she hadn't brought the topic up again. Here they were finally enjoying some cordiality. Leave it to her to ruin it.

"Jess," he began. The way he said her name sent a shiver through her she hoped he didn't notice. "You have to understand why I'm against such an idea."

"Perhaps you could let her make the decision." She literally bit her tongue after the statement. "I'm sorry. I shouldn't have said that. There's that impulsiveness again."

"Don't apologize. It appears we both seem to say things to each other that are perhaps better left unsaid."

"Perhaps."

He let out a deep sigh. "Well, I should get

back to work. I won't be able to get much done later today seeing as Elise has the night off."

Jess blinked in surprise and turned back to face him. "She does?"

He laughed. "Don't look so surprised. Contrary to the initial impression I've obviously given you, I do cut my employees some slack and give them time off once in a while."

Employee.

She couldn't help the thrill that seemed to suddenly lift her heart at those words. Sounded as if Elise was the little girl's nanny. Not a girlfriend at all. And certainly not his wife.

Not that it made an iota of difference as far as she was concerned. She'd discovered the hard way that when it came to relationships, Jess still had a lot to learn about herself—between her spoiled engagement and her uncharacteristic fling. Something told her that when it came to Jordan Paydan, the third time would definitely *not* be the charm.

She gave him a small wave of goodbye as he walked out of the room. What he'd just revealed about this Elise didn't necessarily even mean he was single. Still, the revelation made her giddier than she would care to admit.

* * *

The figures on his spreadsheet floated across his vision in a blurry mess of numbers. He'd never had this much trouble focusing. His mind kept wandering to the woman upstairs busily painting on his sister's bedroom wall. He really should have planned this better. Every cell of his being vibrated with the awareness that they were alone in the house together. Elise and Sonya weren't due back for several more hours.

There was no explainable reason he found himself so attracted to her. For all he knew, Jess was taken. Women like her weren't typically found wanting of suitors. Though she was nothing like the women Jordan himself usually dated, not that he'd ever been terribly serious with anyone. Nor could he entertain such an idea now.

He'd just spent the better part of a year watching his father being utterly betrayed by his wife. She'd proven how disloyal she was when Jordan's dad had gotten sick. His own most recent relationship had floundered as soon as the young lady had learned he'd become the guardian of a little girl. Though she'd used the term "saddled." No, Jordan was in no place in his life right now to embark on any kind of relationship after the past several months.

Besides, his work and his little sister had to be the prime focus of all of his attention right now. With Sonya, there was too much at stake. He'd already done wrong by her on an astronomical level. He didn't need any kind of distraction. Certainly not a distraction in the way of a perky, bohemian artist with olive skin and rich dark brown hair. He found himself wondering, not for the first time, how that thick luxurious hair would feel if he were to run his fingers through it. If he tugged it gently to bring her face closer to his, to finally reach for that kiss.

Whoa.

So not where he needed his thoughts to wander toward. Not when said artist was literally a floor above him. It would be so easy to come up with an excuse to go check on her again. And he was tempted. Oh, so very tempted. He forced himself to look back down at the spreadsheet, knowing full well he wasn't going to be accomplishing much.

An hour later his assumption proved correct. He'd barely made a dent in his workload. A soft knock sounded from the other side of his office door.

Jess. No one else was home. He stood and opened the door for her.

She granted him a small smile. Saints above. How did a woman manage to look so tempting in paint-covered overalls and a do-rag bandanna wrapped around her head? Not that the rag was doing much to maintain any control of her unruly locks.

"Sorry to interrupt," she said. "I just wanted to let you know that I've finished."

Jordan hadn't been expecting the feeling of disappointment that meandered through his gut at the announcement. Nor did he anticipate wondering when he would see her next.

"Oh. Well, thanks. Let me just grab my checkbook."

But she stopped him with a hand to his chest before he could turn away. The contact sent a surge of heat through his core. As if reading his errant mind, she pulled away in haste.

"No, don't do that."

"Do you prefer an electronic transfer of funds?"

She shook her head. "No. I mean I won't accept any money. It was a labor of love. Truly. I'm happy to know Sonya liked it and hopefully she'll enjoy it even more with the additions made today."

Jordan felt a moment of uncertainty. Should he insist? He'd never had anyone turn down a fee for rendered services before. The original artwork was one thing, but he'd asked her to come by this afternoon and add to it.

She smiled at his confusion. "It really isn't necessary, Jordan. You needn't waste another thought on it."

What manner of sorceress was this young lady? She beguiled him. Did something to his senses he wasn't familiar with nor prepared for. Under any other circumstances, despite their clear differences and incompatibility, he might have asked her out. Maybe something as simple as having her show him around this new town he found himself in. And then at the end of the day, they could share a bottle of wine over a cozy candlelit dinner. Then see where things led.

Just. Stop.

Mere moments ago he'd been reminding himself of all the reasons he shouldn't entertain such thoughts about Jess—or any other woman for that matter.

"I don't know what to say. I feel like I should pay for all the time and effort you put in."

Her eyes narrowed on his face. "I assure you, it isn't necessary in this case. Like I said, I refuse to be paid for a task I initiated and loved doing."

He'd never actually thought about it that way; wasn't sure if it even made much sense. "If you're certain," he said, giving her a chance to change her mind once more.

"I am. I wouldn't cash a check if you gave me one."

Several awkward moments ensued. Neither one of them seemed to know what to say next. Though he felt like kicking himself, he desperately didn't want her to walk out the door just yet.

"Do you need help gathering your things?" He finally managed to speak a coherent question.

"Uh… Thanks but I've already loaded everything into my car."

"Oh. I guess—I guess you're all set, then."

She glanced away, a rosy glow appearing on her cheeks.

But then they both spoke at once, over each other.

"I can see myself out." Just as Jordan said, "I'll walk you to your car."

Okay, now the air felt really awkward. He was a successful, accomplished businessman for heaven's sake. He gave professional presentations and delivered talks to some of the most prominent people in the industry. And here he was stammering, trying to talk to a woman he'd just barely met.

He had to get a grip. And he had to stop focusing on how her curves filled out what should have been a completely unflattering denim outfit. Or how her nose seemed to have just the perfect number of light freckles that he only just now noticed.

This was getting ridiculous. He shook off the wayward thoughts. There was no use for them. He was bound to run into her from time to time. Especially considering Sonya would no doubt participate in many activities at the community center where Jess worked. But he would leave it at that. He owed it to his little sister to make her the number one priority right now. After all, if it wasn't for him, that precious little girl could still very well have her hearing intact.

"I should probably get back to work, then," he told her then watched her walk out without another word.

She certainly was leading a glamorous, adventurous life, Jess thought with sarcasm as she settled onto her couch and pulled her tablet out to find a movie to stream. Unlike her mother.

Martha's Vineyard had its fair share of pubs and restaurants. There was plenty to do to socialize, particularly in the summer. She'd been invited to head out to one of those spots with a couple of friends in her apartment building. She'd declined. This suited her just fine. Lately, she was getting tired of the weekend routine of staying up all night then missing half the next day sleeping in. Anyway, she needed some downtime. Her emotions had been on a proverbial roller-coaster ride since Jordan Paydan had stridden into town.

Some strange sorcery must have come into play just then because her tablet lit up with a notification of an incoming call. To her surprise, it was Jordan. Probably calling to give her feedback on Sonya's reaction to the completed diorama. Her mouth went dry and she took a quick sip of water before she could answer.

"Hello," she spoke into her phone.

"I hope I'm not calling at an inconvenient time," his smooth, baritone voice asked over the tiny speaker.

Jess glanced down at the capri sweats she wore and her thinned-out ratty T-shirt. Then she glanced at the pint of mint chocolate chip she planned on as her dinner.

"No. Not at all."

"We were wondering if you were busy later. If you had plans for this evening?"

They were? It took effort to keep her voice from stammering when she answered. "Nothing terribly exciting or urgent," she managed to say. Quite an understatement that was. Her date with the streaming service notwithstanding.

There had to be some explanation for this phone call. Perhaps it wasn't even happening. Maybe she was just dreaming it. It was the only theory that made sense.

"Excellent. See, you and I were sort of wrong about Sonya's reaction to your artwork."

Jess's heart sank. That explained everything. He was calling because his sister was less thrilled, apparently wanted something changed.

"Uh, we were?"

"She wasn't just happy with it. She was thrilled."

"Oh!" Relief surged through her chest. "I'm so happy to hear that."

His amusement at her reaction was clear in his voice when he spoke again. "She asked to thank you in person. Like immediately. Any chance you can join us for dinner?"

The offer was so unexpected, Jess was glad she'd put her glass down on the coffee table. No doubt she would have dropped it. "Dinner?"

He hesitated. "We'll understand if you'd rather pass—"

"No! I mean, I didn't have any plans for dinner at all. Other than the ice cream. Mint chocolate chip. Which isn't really a dinner, but sometimes a girl just needs to relax with a creamy frozen treat. Plus, it's from Bimby's down the street. Have you been there yet? The best ice cream this side of the Atlantic. And they have all sorts of fun activities. Mini-golf, bumper boats. You should really go. Even a petting zoo!" Oh, dear Lord, now she was rambling like a madwoman.

Thank goodness he couldn't see the redness that was sure to be coloring her cheeks. He'd just so completely thrown her off guard. Not that she ever felt fully calm or collected when it came to this man.

He chuckled once more. "We'll be sure to check it out. As for tonight, I've just fired up the grill, then Sonya's going to help me throw together a salad. It should all be ready by the time you get here."

Jess knew she should decline, knew that graciously turning down his invite would be a good idea. An even better idea would be to resolve to try and avoid Jordan Paydan as much as humanly possible.

And it wasn't like she was in any state of dress to be seen out in public, in a ratty T-shirt with even rattier capri sweats and fuzzy socks. Why on earth couldn't she be one of those women who stayed dressed and ready for anything? Rather than one who threw on any old top and a pair of sweats at the first opportunity? Again, so unlike her mom. Jacinda was always ready to go, no matter what the situation called for. Not this again. How many times a day did she have to remind herself not to compare herself to her mother? She'd learned long ago that no one really compared to the woman, least of all her only child. For one, Jacinda wouldn't dream of living full-time on an island off the Massachusetts coast where most people only came on vacation.

In the end, her self-will utterly failed her. "I'm looking forward to it," she replied into the phone on a resigned sigh then made her way to the small bathroom of her apartment. "Thanks for the invite."

"Don't mention it. It's the least we can do. Especially considering you refused any sort of payment for all your hard work."

There it was. A reminder that she couldn't read too much into this invite. Jordan was simply being polite and trying to find a way to thank her since she'd refused his offer of payment. Nothing more than that.

"I can be there in about half an hour if that works."

"Great. I'll let Sonya know. She'll be happy to see you."

He'd just told her that Sonya would be happy to see her. Not Jordan. Again, it would be silly of her to think otherwise, even for a moment.

"Oh, and Jess?" he asked before she'd disconnected.

"Yes?"

"Bring the ice cream. I've always loved mint chocolate chip."

CHAPTER FOUR

JORDAN COULDN'T QUITE recall when he'd actually become an impulsive man. For that was what extending the dinner invite to Jess had been: completely impulsive. But the look on his baby sister's face when she'd seen Jess's completed castle had sent a bolt of emotion through him he hadn't been ready for.

Jess was responsible for that look. So when Sonya said she wished Jess hadn't left before she could tell her thank you, he hadn't allowed himself to think too much about what he wanted to do. He wanted Jess to share the evening with them, one of their first few evenings in their new home without the stress and hassle of unpacking or trying to get fully settled. The little girl had been through so much in such a short period of time, it touched Jordan's heart when she did manage a genuine, heartfelt smile.

He threw a dozen prepared kebabs on the patio's built-in circular stone grill and turned to really study his new backyard for the first time. His new environment was so different than the high-rise luxury apartment he'd called home until just recently.

An inground crystal-blue pool complete with two cascading waterfalls marked the central centerpiece of a lushly green outdoor space. A gray brick patio area led to a double screen door to the kitchen of the main house. The caretakers' cottage, which Elise occupied, could be seen about an acre away. The grill and a built-in fire pit sat between the sitting area and the pool.

Would Jess like it?

Funny, he'd never particularly felt the need to impress a woman before. An outside observer may find it coldhearted, but the women he'd been involved with in the past weren't ones he'd felt terribly invested in emotionally; his relationships were based on not much more than mutual attraction.

He glanced at the expensive Italian Frascati sitting in the ice bucket by the glass dining table. He'd spent an exorbitant amount of time in the gourmet wine shop earlier this evening picking out a bottle he thought would suit what little he knew of Jess's tastes. So yeah, that was something of a new experience, as well.

He was definitely trying to impress her; there was no denying it. Nor was there any denying of the bolt of pleasure that shot through his center when he heard her voice behind him. He turned to find her walking through the kitchen screen door with Sonya trailing behind her.

"Something smells mouthwateringly delicious. I hope it's okay. Sonya let me in when she noticed me outside the front door."

No, he didn't mind at all. Was immensely pleased she was here and would be spending the evening with them.

"Of course not. Come in. Have a seat. The kebabs should be ready momentarily."

Sonya was beaming. She pulled her chair close to the one Jordan had pulled out for Jess and sat right next to her. Hard to explain exactly why the little girl had taken such a swift liking to the young artist teacher. Perhaps they were kindred souls or spirits who had called to each other. So what was his own excuse?

"Thanks for coming out," he told her.

She gave him a small smile before answering. "Thank you for the invite. To be honest, I never thought I'd be having dinner here, in this house."

"Oh? You were familiar with the house from before?"

Jess chuckled as she settled into her seat. "You're kidding, right? This place is known throughout town. The old Tallard mansion. Everyone's been wondering about its next occupant ever since the Tallards moved to Panama City last year."

So maybe she was impressed. Only, it had nothing to do with him. He would have to do something about that.

"They shall wonder no more."

She looked around. "The patio additions are new. And so are the waterfalls."

"I had them add a few new touches."

"Very nice," she repeated. Damn it, he should have thought to ask her to bring a bathing suit. The night was pleasantly warm and the pool water heated to the perfect temp. He found himself wondering what she would look like in a formfitting bikini. She looked like the type who might have a belly button ring. And a small tattoo somewhere discreet, maybe on her inner thigh. He had to shake those images away before it was too late.

Sonya continued to smile as the two spoke. Within minutes they'd each filled their plates and had begun to eat.

"You appear to be a man of many talents, Mr. Paydan," Jess declared. "Quite the cook based on this meal."

Jordan grunted. "Hardly. The kebabs were premade at the butcher and Sonya suggested crispy French bread to go with it all. I'm going to have to figure out meals going forward. I'll have to find a live-in chef or a meal delivery service like we had in Manhattan. Or we'll be having kebabs every night unless we want to starve."

Whether Sonya heard the gist of what he'd said or she was reacting to his expression, he couldn't be sure. But she giggled with amusement. She was truly enjoying herself. When was the last time that had happened?

Jess nodded. "Clara mentioned that your mom had moved to New York after leaving the island. The vineyard must seem like a far cry from Manhattan," she supplied.

"It's going to be a bit of an adjustment. But

my mother grew up here. And I think it's a better environment for Sonya." The ever-present feeling of guilt clogged his throat and he had to clear it before he choked on it.

"That's why you made such a drastic move?"

He nodded. "I should have done so as soon as I found myself the guardian of a small child."

"Sounds as if it was somewhat unexpected." Jess shifted in her seat. "If you don't mind my asking, how did that come about? I'm sorry if it's not something you like to discuss."

Did he mind talking about it? He certainly hadn't spoken of their circumstances much with many others. Though every one in New York's social circles was well aware of his tale. It had made all the rounds in the city papers. He found himself wanting to share the story with her, though she was barely more than a stranger at this point.

He put his fork down and began to tell her.

Jess wanted very badly to reach out and stroke Jordan's hand in comfort as he spoke. Sonya had finished eating and was now lying on a lounge chair by the pool, fully engrossed in a picture book. As accomplished and successful a man as Jordan was, he must have been completely taken by shock by the circumstances that had led him to where he was today. But Jess didn't know him well enough to guess as to whether he would welcome such a move. She hardly knew him at all. So why did she feel so touched by what he was describing to her about all the turmoil he'd been dealt in the past few years?

"I lost my mother as a teen," he told her. "She became ill and never recovered." The sorrow in his voice as he spoke of the loss had tears stinging her eyes.

"She's a bit of a legend around here," Jess said. "Local girl who moved on to become an international fashion model. Then married a successful American tycoon."

Jordan swallowed. "They lived a fairy-tale life until hers ended. In a way, my father never really recovered either after she was gone."

"I'm so sorry, Jordan." The words felt so useless as she uttered them.

"I tried to keep myself busy and distracted with school. I'd been attending an exclusive boarding school in Rhode Island. My father insisted it was better for me to maintain my regular routine. So I went back even though I worried about leaving him."

"Your father's concern for you overrode his grief."

"He grieved a long while. So it surprised me when he remarried over a decade later. Sonya's mother is everything my mom was not."

"How so?"

"She was a model, as well. They met during fashion week at a charity event. That's where any similarities end between her and my mother. She barely acknowledged her child, leaving her in the care of my father and an ever-revolving stream of nannies. I never risked insulting my father by mentioning it, but I have little doubt that Sonya's conception was merely a ploy to snare a wealthy husband."

Jess grasped for the right words, but they failed her.

"For her, their marriage was mostly about the money and the lifestyle," Jordan continued. "And the constant partying."

"I see." He didn't even realize just how well.

"Then my dad got sick himself about three years ago," Jordan continued. "Sonya was just three."

"Oh, Jordan. I'm so sorry for your loss," she could only repeat.

"He fought his illness as long as he could, until about six months ago. Sonya's mom barely stopped partying long enough to visit her husband's bedside. I was the one there with him during those final days."

It didn't take a genius to figure out what had happened as his father lay dying. "He asked you to take care of Sonya because he didn't trust her mother to."

"Give the lady a prize," Jordan said softly with zero humor behind the lighthearted words. He looked away to where his little sister lay flipping the pages of her book. "Her mother didn't even pretend to try and fight me. As long as she got her share of the Paydan fortune, which she did. In fact, she didn't even bother to hide her relief at not having to deal with her own child."

A deathbed wish. Of course, Jordan had to accept the responsibility suddenly being thrust upon him. Though a lot of lesser men might not have. A lot of men would have just told the dying parent simply what they wanted to hear and then not followed through.

Jordan was not one of those men.

He suddenly pushed his chair back and stood. "Well, enough talk of the past. Let's go get that ice cream, shall we?"

He was clearly done talking for now. Jess wasn't one to push, even if Jordan's recounting of his history had touched several nerves about her own. How different would her own life had turned out if only one responsible relative had taken her in permanently? Rather than the ever-changing chain of homes she'd been tossed to, one after another. Not one person had come through for her the way Jordan had for his little sister.

Well, it was all water under the bridge now. Past history. She'd moved on and made a real life for herself. There was a lot to be said for that. Even if there had been quite a few bumps along the way. And even if it got a little lonely once in a while. She glanced at Jordan from the side of her eye.

Sonya noticed her brother's movement and came over to the table. Without another word, the three of them walked into the kitchen. Jordan opened the freezer door then turned to look at the two of them with a blank expression.

That was when Jess noticed the ice cream on the counter. Only now it was less ice cream and more a gooey puddle of white speckled with dark pieces of chocolate where it had leaked out of its container as it melted.

"I guess we forgot to put it in the freezer."

Sonya sniffled with sadness as she studied the mess. She was on the verge of tears. How could she have been so stupid? She'd just been so nervous at the prospect of seeing Jordan again that she'd simply handed the pint to the little girl without making sure it was put away.

"I'm so sorry, Sonya," she said, kneeling down to look the little girl in the eye. Yep, she was definitely tearing up.

"Nonsense," Jordan said above them. "You're our guest. You didn't even know where our fridge is. I'm the one who should apologize."

Jess looked up to find him rubbing a hand down his face. Then suddenly, to her surprise, he broke into a wide grin. "There's only one way to fix this," he declared.

"What would that be?"

"Well, we can't go without dessert after a meal like that. What kind of host would that make me?"

"I'm the one who left the ice cream to melt. I suppose I can whip up some cookies if you have the ingredients. I make a mean chocolate chip."

He shook his head. "I'm afraid we don't have ingredients for much of anything."

What was he getting at, then?

"You mentioned you got the ice cream from a well-known town attraction. And that Sonya and I had to check it out sometime. What better time than the present?"

Without waiting for her answer, he picked up his little sister and set her down on the counter. Then he proceeded to sign and gesture. Jess had to bite back a laugh when he made a motion of licking an ice cream cone.

The scene before Jess sent an undeniably clear revelation through her mind. Though their first impressions of each other had been less than idyllic, and though she'd only known him a few short days, she seemed to be growing fonder of Jordan Paydan than she wanted to.

She had no idea what to do about it.

The place was a madhouse. Jordan took a look around at the hustle of activity around him as they made their way to the ice cream line. The very long ice cream line. A group of kids ran past them and he noticed the look of longing that passed over Sonya's face. Hopefully, she would meet some of these very same children when she started the swimming classes at the center.

Jess was right. This place offered so much more than ice cream. A volleyball net was set up a few feet behind the ice cream shack with what seemed to be a very intense game. Several diners sat under a large tent full of picnic tables. A couple of teenage boys were tossing a Frisbee in the field adjacent. Across the parking lot was a full-fledged mini-golf setup. Bimby's was packed with adults and children alike. Not to mention some livestock. Was that a chicken that just ran by his feet?

"Wow," was all he could manage as they stopped at the end of the line.

Jess laughed at his reaction to all the activity. "This is relatively slow for a Saturday evening," she said, surprising him.

"I'd hate to see what busy looks like for this place."

"We'd still be in the parking lot trying to make our way to the ice cream line."

Several more people came to stand behind them. "We could be here all night waiting." Though he could think of worse things than enjoying a pleasant evening chatting with the woman standing beside him. He was truly enjoying her company and had been since she'd walked onto his patio a few hours earlier. In fact, the thought struck that he didn't want this evening to end. Stunning, really. Considering his usual idea of a good evening would be an elegant dinner in a five-star restaurant somewhere Midtown followed by drinks and slow dancing on one of the rooftop clubs that he liked to frequent on dates.

He would certainly enjoy those things with the woman next to him.

Stop it.

This was a simple outing for ice cream. He had to try and ignore the unwelcome attraction to a woman he had absolutely nothing in common with. Nor did he have anything to offer. Not at this stage in his life.

"The lines actually go by pretty quickly," Jess

answered him. "Bimby's scoopers are experts at ice cream efficiency."

She was right. In hardly any time at all, they had each received their orders and were sitting at one of the picnic tables. Sonya's sundae was the size of her head and she was making a complete mess. There was no way she would finish it. But Jordan hadn't had the heart to tell her no when she'd pointed to the special scribbled out on the chalkboard.

"What do you think?" Jess asked him, lifting her cone and then gesturing to all the activity around them.

"I think so far you've proven yourself a commendable tour guide," he answered. "Who knows when we would have heard about this place if it wasn't for you."

She laughed. "It was one of the first places I visited when I moved to the vineyard."

He studied her. There was so much about her he didn't know. He found he was terribly curious to find out.

"How long have you lived here?"

"About three years," she answered.

How did someone like her end up living here

full-time? She must have sensed his nonverbal question because she went on to answer it.

"My college roommate grew up on Martha's Vineyard. I accompanied her on some of her holiday visits back home. After graduation she moved back and I came here with her." She took a lick of her ice cream cone and he had to look away in order to continue focusing on her words. "It was only supposed to be temporary. Just for one summer. I was enrolled in graduate school in Boston. I attended just two semesters before realizing I'd made a mistake. Found it wasn't really my calling."

"So you came back here."

Jess nodded. "It was the only place that had ever really felt like home. Though Kelly has since moved on," Jess added. "Out to the West Coast with a toddler and another baby on the way."

"You sound as if you miss her," he said in response to the faraway look that had appeared in her eyes.

"I do. Her parents still have me over for dinner every Sunday that I can make it."

"Standing invitation?"

She nodded. "That's right. That's how this

island operates. One of the qualities that drew me to it."

There was clearly a story there. As much as he wanted to ask, Jordan didn't want to push. He himself had shared enough for one night. And though part of him felt good about getting some of it off his chest, another part felt drained, even a little exposed.

The chicken strutted by their table again and Sonya giggled at it. Or maybe that was a totally different chicken. Damned if he knew. He was just glad his little sister appeared to be having some fun at long last. Moving to this town had to work out for them.

He glanced over at the woman sitting next to him. She was motioning to Sonya that she had a little chocolate on her nose and was laughing. She leaned over to wipe it when Sonya tried but kept missing the spot. Little did she know, she had a bit of chocolate smeared on her own cheek.

Jordan couldn't help but imagine all sorts of ways he could help her clean it off.

CHAPTER FIVE

"WHAT IS THAT godforsaken noise?" Jordan asked as they finished up their ice cream. Well, he and Jess had finished theirs anyway. His little sister had more or less taken a few bites then smeared some of it around in her cardboard bowl as she'd gotten it all over herself and her clothes.

"What particular noise are you speaking of?" Jess asked. She had a point. There was a lot going on around them. But he was certain he heard a low-level humming coming from a distance behind the dining tent.

"That constant buzzing that's always in the background. That noise."

She stood and motioned for him and Sonya to do so, as well. "Here. I'll show you."

Sonya didn't hesitate. She jumped up and rushed to Jess's side. The buzzing grew louder as they walked around the tent then behind it. A pungent scent of exhaust filled the air and grew stronger with each step they took. As soon as they turned the bend, he saw it. A small lake surrounded by lush greenery and shrubs. Another long line of people snaked around it. The lake was being used as a venue for gasoline engine bumper boats.

Sonya squealed in delight and clasped her hands together.

Several of the boats were on the water at the moment, manned by kids and adults alike. All of them trying to bump into each other hard enough to either topple the other occupant or at least get them fairly wet.

"You weren't kidding about this place," Jordan said. "It really does have everything."

"Are you up for it?" she asked with a taunting undertone.

"Clearly, that was a challenge."

"Maybe."

He gestured toward the line. "Lead the way, madam. Though I feel compelled to warn you how out of your league you will be once we get on that water."

"Oh, yeah?"

"Yes. I happen to be an avid boater with years of experience."

She laughed at him. “These aren’t the kind of boats you’re used to, sir. I must be the one to warn you. Through my three or so summers on Martha’s Vineyard, I’ve become a bumper boat master sailor. With countless trophies under my belt.”

“A master, huh?”

She nodded. “That’s correct. I have a bit of a reputation around town.”

“Nice try,” he teased. “Your intimidation tactics won’t work on me, I’m afraid.”

“Let the record show then that I gave you ample opportunity to back out,” she said with another laugh. “Prepare to be humiliated, my dear sir.”

“I suppose we shall see, won’t we?” He placed a hand against the small of her back and led her toward the line. The warmth of her skin under his palm sent a responding warmth through his skin. Her cropped shirt was just short enough that he could feel a small expanse of her skin. Smooth, silky. She had to feel that way all over, he had no doubt.

The three of them stood in line for just a few minutes before it was their turn. He turned to pick Sonya up and deposit her in a boat. But when he went to step into it, his sister shook her head. Then she pointed to Jess.

She wanted Jess to ride with her.

Jordan wasn't sure whether to be touched or feel wary. Though Elise was a competent and efficient caregiver to Sonya, the woman wasn't one to show much affection. Clearly, Sonya was sensing an underlying vibe from Jess that drew her. And it seemed to be happening quickly.

Don't really blame you, kid.

But it was something he had to think about. Her life had been altered so completely and so often over the past couple of years, even the slightest further upheaval could be harmful.

He held his hand out toward Jess and she complied without any hesitation. She felt light in his arms as he lifted her. For the briefest instant, their eyes met as he held her. An electricity crackled between them that she had to have noticed, as well. Wordlessly, he assisted Jess into the boat his sister occupied then found one for himself and climbed in.

There was no clear victor by the time they each got out. All three of them were soaking wet.

Sonya was laughing so hard, Jordan wondered if she might actually topple over. He couldn't recall the last time he'd heard her laugh like that. Then he looked in Jess's direction and he had to suck in his breath. Now that her clothes were wet, they clung to her like a second skin. And they accentuated every luscious curve. The bikini he'd imagined her in earlier couldn't have been as enticing as the picture she made right now. She shook some of the water out of her hair and he had to clench his fist to keep from reaching over and running his fingers through her thick, rich curls.

He bit out a curse under his breath. He had no business having such thoughts, here of all places.

"Thank goodness it's a warm night," Jess said through her laughter.

"They could add to their profits if they sold towels."

"We should put that idea in the suggestion box." Suddenly, she stilled and put a hand to her mouth.

"What is it?"

"It just occurred to me that we'll have to crawl into your car soaking wet. Jordan, I'm so sorry. That car has to be terribly expensive."

He brushed off her concern with a wave of his hand. Truth be told, he had other things to worry about right now than the leather bucket seats of his convertible getting a little damp.

For one, he had to figure out how to avoid looking at the appealing woman that stood beside him looking dangerously sexy in her clingy, wet clothing.

"Don't worry about that," he reassured her.

"Still, we should at least try to dry out a little before we get back in."

That suited him just fine. Again, he found he didn't want the time to end.

Jess knew it was simply a matter of time before they ran into someone she knew. It was a common phenomenon at Bimby's. No real surprise given the popularity of the place and the nature of the community that housed it. They'd decided to take a walk around the establishment in the hopes that the dry evening air would at least make some small progress in lessening how wet their clothes were. Sure enough, she heard a familiar voice behind them calling out her name.

"Jess? I thought that was you." When she

reached them, Clara had a toddler in tow. Her granddaughter. The older woman took in the sight of the three of them and her mouth curved into a smile. "I see you've all been on the bumper boats."

"Hello, Clara," Jess greeted her then waved to the child with her, who waved back with a toothy grin. "You remember Jordan and Sonya."

Clara's smile grew wider. "Of course."

"I'm just showing the two of them around Bimby's," Jess explained after the preliminary round of hellos were out of the way. The two children stood shyly trying to avoid looking at each other.

"Oh, how lovely!" Clara declared. "You can't find a better local to show you around, Jordan."

"I have no doubt about that."

Clara leaned down to tousle Sonya's hair. "And what about you? Are you having fun?" Without waiting for Sonya's answer, Clara continued. "Teddy and I were just about to head to the petting zoo." She pointed to the sign behind them on the gated enclosure that housed the farm animals. "Would you like to come with us? My other grandchildren will be there, too."

Sonya looked up to her brother for approval.

Oh, Clara. She wasn't even trying to hide her intent to try and get Jess and Jordan alone.

Jordan signed something slowly to Sonya, who nodded slowly.

"You have a taker," he told Clara, who then took Sonya by the hand. Jess and Jordan could only watch as they walked away and toward the big metal gate.

Jess let out a long sigh. "Clara is not very subtle."

"So I see."

"She means well."

"I suppose she does."

Several awkward moments ensued where they simply stood watching other people stroll by. This was just silly, Jess thought. They were both adults. They could certainly find a way to pass some time together while they waited.

"Carla has six grandchildren," she announced, simply to make conversation. "She's been married to her high school sweetheart for over forty years."

Jordan looked off into the distance, silent for a moment. Finally, he spoke. "How lucky for her. For both of them."

"Lucky?"

He shrugged. "To have found the person they each wanted to spend the rest of their lives with. And have grandchildren together."

A grim tone had settled into his voice. He was clearly speaking from personal experience. But her gut told her he wasn't speaking about himself. Maybe that was just wishful thinking on her part. She asked anyway. "Are you thinking of your mom and dad?"

Jordan folded his arms in front of his chest before he spoke. "I guess my parents were lucky, too. For a while anyway. My dad certainly wasn't as fortunate the next time love came around knocking for him." The way he pronounced the word *love* had a distinct undertone of disdain. "I've seen a successful marriage that crumbled due to illness, and I've seen a disastrous one that should have never happened in the first place. One has to wonder if the risk is even worth it."

He gave his head a brisk shake as if to clear it. Jess didn't know quite what to say to his last comment. After all, she'd had the same notion more than once since her breakup. Gary's utter rejection once she'd made her decision to change careers had sent her self-confidence stumbling several notches. It had taken her some time to convince herself that she was simply enough, by being exactly who she was. But to hear the cynical words spoken out loud the way that Jordan had phrased them, filled her heart with sadness.

The conversation had suddenly turned too deep, too serious. The air around them seemed to grow heavy and loaded. An idea struck her about how to possibly lighten the mood. She turned to him. "The contest with the bumper boats could certainly be considered a draw."

He blinked at her. "I beg your pardon?"

"I mean, we're pretty much even after my challenge."

"And?"

"Clearly, we need another test of sorts to settle the matter."

"Not that I'm ready to concede anything, but what do you have in mind?"

She had to giggle at his serious tone. "That I have another challenge for you."

"I'm listening."

"I bet I can beat you at mini-golf."

His dark gray eyes filled with mirth. "You're on."

She beat him soundly on the first hole. But apparently, he was just warming up. By the time they got to hole three, she was already up by five strokes. To his credit, he only taunted her once about it. Luckily, they hadn't placed any kind of wager.

"How are you sinking so many holes in one?" she demanded in exasperation.

Jordan gave her a sheepish grin. "I have an admission to make."

"What's that?"

"I golf regularly. Started when I was barely a preteen. Mini-golf isn't any different than putting on the green."

She should have guessed. Someone of Jordan's wealth and status probably had access to some of the most elite courses on the East Coast. No wonder he was beating her so badly. But her pathetic score did nothing to dampen her fun. In fact, this was the most fun she could remember having in quite a while.

The next hole took them through an artificial cave. Jess suddenly found herself in a tight, dark space completely alone with the most enigmatic man she'd ever encountered. In an instant everything else around them faded into the background. Only the two of them seemed to exist.

Jordan was so close, she was certain he could hear the increased pounding of her heart. So close that it would be so easy to lean toward him with a clear invitation. So easy to ask him to kiss her.

Heat and excitement curled deep in her belly at the thought. What might it feel like to have his lips on hers? She could smell the subtle scent of his aftershave. That same smoky, woodsy scent she was now beginning to associate with the man.

Was he wondering about kissing her, too?

The breath seemed to be leaving her chest in gasps. He had to notice the effect he was having on her. Was probably too much of a gentleman to acknowledge it. Oh, but a part of her so wished he would.

She knew Jordan was far out of her league. From what Clara had told her so far, he was successful and accomplished. Together enough to not only be in charge of an international finance business but also for a little girl he'd taken on complete responsibility for.

Whereas she was barely making ends meet with no idea what her plans for the future were, aside from a part-time teaching gig and various artistic projects that paid if and only if they came to be.

They were from two completely different worlds. She had no business being attracted to him. And she certainly had no business acting on it anyway.

Even in the dark, she could read hunger on his face. Desire for her. He was attracted to her, too. The idea made her giddy and downright terrified at the same time. How she had ended up here she had to wonder. A few short days ago she hadn't even known Jordan Paydan existed. Now she couldn't imagine going even one day without thinking about him.

It wouldn't take much for him to kiss her. She had no doubt that if she so much as leaned farther toward him, he would take her up on the clear invitation. But this was all so confusing. They'd only just met, for heaven's sake.

She made herself pull away.

Finally, Jordan cleared his throat and stepped

back, as well. He was barely tall enough to fit inside the makeshift cave. They had to get out of here for more reasons than one.

"I…uh…" Jess stammered like a confused toddler. She'd never felt at such a loss for words before.

"I think it's your turn," Jordan said simply, sparing her the need to try and complete her sentence.

Not that she really had any idea of what she'd been planning to say.

Dear Lord, he'd almost kissed her back there. Jordan rubbed a hand down his face and tried to compose himself as Jess returned their golf clubs to the teenage worker at the mini-golf stand. What had he been thinking? The fact was he hadn't been. The first half hour of being alone with her and he'd almost lost control.

It absolutely could not happen again. He'd just have to be sure never to be alone with her anymore. Starting right now.

As soon as she approached him, he said as much. "We've probably been gone too long."

Her breath seemed to puff out in little gasps. Was that because of his effect on her? If only he could test that theory by taking her into his arms, despite the myriad people around them. If only he could kiss her like he'd so badly wanted to in that silly plaster toy cave.

"Of course." She nodded. "Though Sonya's definitely in good hands. Clara was a teacher for over twenty years and has all those grandchildren she helps take care of."

He knew all that. It had come up in the center's office when he'd signed his sister up for the gymnast classes. He would have never let Sonya go with the woman if he hadn't been confident of her skill level. "Nevertheless."

"You're right. They've probably run out of animals to pet."

But they were interrupted before they'd gone far.

A tall and fit gentleman with dark blond hair jogged up behind Jess and playfully tapped her on the shoulder. When she turned to him, he gave her a bright smile. But the look he glanced in Jordan's direction appeared less than cordial.

"Travis. Hi."

The man didn't tear his gaze off him even as he responded to the greeting. Whoever this Travis was, he wasn't terribly thrilled at seeing Jess here with him. A spear of jealousy shot through his chest.

"Have you been here long?" Jess asked in a clear attempt to simply make conversation as things appeared to swiftly be turning to the awkward.

"Just got here," Travis answered. "I'm really glad I ran into you."

Jess indicated Jordan with a head nod in his direction. "This is Jordan Paydan. He just moved to the island recently."

The handshake that ensued held absolutely zero friendliness or pleasantness of any degree.

"Are you showing him around or something?" Travis wanted to know.

Jordan resisted the strong urge to ask him why he thought it was any of his business.

Except maybe it was.

A disquieting thought occurred to him. He knew so little of Jess. Despite an almost surreal and inexplicable attraction, she was barely more than a stranger. He'd speculated earlier that she might be in a relationship with a man. But now that one stood before them, given the way he was looking at her with nothing short of possession in his eyes, the notion disturbed Jordan more than he cared to admit. Much more. His hands clenched into tight fists at his sides.

He was jealous.

Of all the foolish… If he'd ever felt the emotion before, he couldn't recall the time. Not when it came to a female, in any case. What in the world was wrong with him? He wasn't even himself when it came to this woman.

He didn't give Jess a chance to answer Travis's question. He spoke before she could. "Yes, Jess has been nice enough to introduce us to one of the town's biggest attractions." He turned to her before continuing. "I'm going to go find the others now. I'll meet you there. Unless you think you may have found another ride back home."

There. He'd given her the out if she wanted to take it. Though he hated the thought that she actually might take it.

Her whiskey-gold eyes narrowed on him, hardened. "Travis was just saying hello. Weren't you?"

Travis merely nodded. He seemed utterly at a loss for what to say. Welcome to the club, pal.

"First of all, my car is parked in your driveway."

She had a point there.

She continued, "Secondly, I'll leave with the person I came here with."

A small, churlish hint of satisfaction hit him as they said their goodbyes and started walking away. Then he reminded himself how he didn't need any of this. He didn't need to feel strange emotions over a woman he'd just met. He didn't need to feel jealous simply because she'd been approached by another man. He had enough on his plate. And he couldn't afford to mess any of it up. Particularly when it came to the well-being of his sister. No, he didn't have the time or the inclination. Look at how his father's life had been shattered. First, when he'd lost the woman he'd loved for over three decades. Then again when he'd been selfishly used by another. Look at all the lives that had been affected in turn. His. Sonya's.

Serious relationships weren't for him. Certainly not now. Probably not ever. And Jess certainly wasn't the type of woman he'd entertain indulging in a meaningless fling with. She deserved more than that.

It was better to cease all this now before Sonya grew more attached. For he had no doubt things were heading in that direction for his little sister.

Inviting Jess over for dinner was a mistake. He should have known better.

"A friend of yours?" he asked when the silence between them had gone awkwardly long during their walk back.

"Yes. As a matter of fact." She answered with a clear bite in her tone.

"Appeared to be a very good friend, in fact."

"My old roommate's brother. I've known him for years." She was clearly speaking through gritted teeth. He'd made her angry. Well, so be it. Not like he was exactly feeling pleasant. Was she trying to say the friendship was purely platonic? If so, he had no doubt it was one-sided. She was blind to the other man's obvious feelings for her. Just meeting the man for a few brief moments and Jordan had been able to see it as clear as the setting sun in the horizon.

Again, none of this was any of his concern. He had to keep reminding himself of that. Yep. Dinner with Jess had definitely been a mistake. He'd be sure to make better decisions in the future as far as she was concerned. After all, he had more than himself to consider now.

He was in charge of a child. One whom he'd already let down in the most unforgivable way imaginable.

To think the evening had started so pleasant and cordial. They'd even had some kind of moment while playing mini-golf. And then Jordan had tried to hoist her off on another man for a ride as soon as he'd had the chance. Sitting in his passenger seat now, the ride back to his place seemed to be taking forever. The only sound in the car was Sonya's rhythmic, steady breathing in the backseat. If she hadn't already fallen asleep back there, she certainly was close.

Well, Jess wasn't going to try and break the silence. Damned if she would be the one to start speaking first. She'd be too tempted to curse if she did.

Finally, they pulled into the paved circular driveway of Jordan's Mediterranean-style mansion complete with plaster columns and an upper balcony above the front double doors. The house was lit up with floodlights now that the sun had set.

Jess got out of the car when Jordan came to

a stop and opened Sonya's car door for her. The child got out rubbing her eyes. Yeah, she was beyond beat. Jess crouched down in front of her as Jordan came to stand a few feet away behind his sister.

"Good night, Sonya. I hope you had fun."

Sonya smiled at her. "Let's get you cleaned up and into bed." Jordan spoke behind them. "Then I'll tuck you in."

But when Jess stood to leave, Sonya grabbed her hand. She seemed to struggle as her mouth quivered. Then floored her by actually speaking. "Jeth do ee."

Jess do it.

Oh, heavens. Jess had never heard the child try to speak until now. And she was doing so to ask Jess to get her ready for bed.

There was no mistaking the shock that flooded over Jordan's features. Well, she was pretty surprised herself. She gave Jordan a questioning look above Sonya's head. She may be mad at him, but she wasn't about to usurp a decision that was clearly his to make. He came to stand by her and touched his sister on the shoulder.

"You're saying you want Jess to help you into bed?"

The little girl didn't hesitate and nodded with solemn determination.

Jordan let out a deep sigh as he rubbed his hand down his face before crouching down in front of his sister. "I'm sure Jess is tired, sport. Why don't we let her be on her way?"

The irritation she'd felt for him earlier fled like a flock of migrant birds. To his credit, Jordan really was trying to do right by Sonya.

The little girl nodded and dropped her chin to her chest, but not before Jess noticed the clear tell of sudden tears in her eyes. *Damn it.*

"Come on, kiddo," Jordan continued, "we don't want to end such a pleasant day on this solemn note, do we?"

Sonya slowly shook her head but didn't look up from staring at her toes. Jordan lifted his head to look at her then. The depth of emotion in his eyes took Jess's breath away. It was tearing him up inside that he had to disappoint his sister. Jess didn't give herself time to think. She gave him a small nod. "It would be my pleasure to help Sonya into bed, if it's okay with you," she said softly, so that only he could hear her.

Gratitude flooded his features and the look he gave her nearly knocked the breath out of her lungs.

Jordan quickly signed to Sonya. This time the little girl gave a wide smile before reaching for Jess's hand. She'd made the right decision, hadn't she? After all, she was simply putting a child to bed after she'd been asked.

Together, the three of them made their way up the front steps and into the house.

CHAPTER SIX

"PLEASE JUST HELP her get as cleaned up as possible," Jordan instructed as they approached the circular stairway. "A bath would be ideal but she's likely to fall asleep in the water as exhausted as she is."

Jess nodded. "Got it."

"After she brushes her teeth, it's just a matter of getting her into bed with a picture book for a few minutes before lights out."

"Sounds simple enough," Jess answered and smiled at Sonya, who seemed to be paying close attention to her older brother's directions.

Jordan rubbed a hand through the thick hair at the top of his head. "I guess I'll just go get some work done while you two are up there."

Jess led Sonya up the stairs and took the opportunity to take a good look at the first floor. She'd just passed through quickly earlier this evening. As she'd expected, Jordan had gone with the eggshell-white paint throughout the whole first floor. Most likely the second floor, as well. The furniture was modern and spotless.

Jordan had mentioned they were all done unpacking. So this was it. The place looked like it could have been put together by a hotel decorator to look as generic as possible. A few pieces of art hung on the walls. Priceless, no doubt. But she saw no photographs. In fact, nothing in the house gave any indication of who lived there or what their personality might be.

The only part of the house that showed any hint of personality was the castle she'd drawn herself in Sonya's room. It had caused a bit of a ruckus at first between her and Jordan, but she was very glad to have done it.

In a matter of minutes, Sonya was cleaned, brushed and dressed in a soft cotton nightie. She settled into the bed and Jess pulled the covers over her.

"Which book will it be?" Jess asked.

Sonya pointed to a hard cardboard-covered book sitting on her nightstand. Her breath caught when Jess picked it up and saw what it was.

Mother Goose.

"Our school play." She did her best to sign out the letters P-L-A-Y.

Sonya nodded.

Jess pointed at Sonya's chest then pointed at the book. "Do you think you might like to be in it, after all? I can talk to your brother."

Though the notion had her palms breaking into a sweat. Given his initial reaction to the suggestion a few days ago and the fact that weren't exactly on the best of terms at the moment, asking Jordan about the play would not be something to look forward to.

But she would do it for Sonya.

The little girl shrugged. Then started to sign. S-C-A… Jess couldn't make out the next letters. Sonya continued with E-D.

Scared. She was telling her she was scared.

"Everyone gets a little frightened to be on stage." Sonya seemed to understand the gist of what she was saying. Then Jess signed O and then K.

They both settled on the mattress and slowly began flipping the thick cardboard pages. She had no idea how much time had passed. So she was surprised to wake up to Jordan's wide smile a couple of hours later with Sonya snuggled tight up against her chest.

Jordan had to admit how torn he felt at the scene that greeted him when he finally stepped into his sister's room after losing track of time while he worked.

Jess had fallen asleep herself. She lay sprawled on the side of Sonya's bed fully clothed on top of the covers.

"I'm so sorry," she whispered as she gingerly stood so as not to wake the child who had nestled up against her. "I guess I was so tired, I couldn't stay awake."

"So it would appear."

She didn't make eye contact as she strode by him out of the bedroom and into the hall. Jordan softly shut the door behind him and turned to where she stood.

She was a disheveled mess. Her clothing had to still be at least damp and clung to her in a wrinkled mess of fabric. Her hair was a pile of unruly curls framing her face and cascading down her shoulders only about half still in the clip. Her cheeks were ruddy and her eyes swollen with sleep.

He thought she looked achingly beautiful.

"I'll just be on my way, I guess. Sorry to have overstayed my welcome."

But he stopped her before she could walk away. He gently took her by the arm and turned her to face him. "Wait."

"What is it, Jordan?"

"It's late. And you're tired. There's no need for you to leave. Spend the night in the guest room. I'd feel better not letting you drive given the hour and your grogginess."

He could see the battle behind her eyes. Jordan didn't want to speculate as to the causes of her hesitation; wouldn't allow himself to read too much into the reaction. She had to know he was simply offering a logical alternative to driving in the middle of the night while she was sleepy.

Logic apparently won out. She hesitated some more before finally blowing out a breath. "I guess it's probably wise to stay."

Before she could change her mind, Jordan showed her the way to the guest suite down the hall.

"Good night, Jordan. Hope you have a pleasant sleep," she said, then slowly shut the door.

He knew full well that wasn't terribly likely. Not with Jess merely a few feet away under the same roof.

The hours that slowly passed until morning only served to prove him right. Jordan spent the night tossing and turning, his mind restless and all too aware of his alluring overnight guest.

When morning finally arrived, it wasn't soon enough. Jordan made his way into the kitchen and immediately plugged in the coffee machine. He wasn't surprised when Jess appeared in the doorway. She looked every bit as tempting as she had last night.

"Thank you for such fine accommodations. I definitely needed the rest."

At least one of them had gotten some sleep, Jordan thought with no small amount of envy. "What kind of host would I be if I didn't offer you a cup of coffee upon awakening?"

She gave him a small, albeit grateful, smile. "I'll take you up on that. I'm not really safe to operate heavy machinery before a hit of caffeine in the morning."

There went his resolution from just yesterday about not inviting Jess to any more activities. But he knew they had to talk before she left.

They couldn't just ignore what had happened last night. Though he wanted nothing more right now than to do just that, he'd never been one to put off things he didn't want to face.

The coffee was brewed in no time and he was soon pouring each of them a tall, steamy mug of the rich Jamaican blend he always had on hand.

"This smells heavenly. Thanks," Jess said before taking a small sip.

"How did Sonya seem last night?" he asked her.

"Tired. Very tired." She ducked her head as if embarrassed. "And apparently, so was I."

"We shouldn't have asked you to stay after such a long day. I apologize."

Jess blinked and looked away. "I'm glad you did. I enjoyed getting Sonya into bed. She's a delightful little girl."

"She's been through a lot. In a very short span of time. I need to be careful with her."

She sucked in a breath before continuing. As if she were weighing her words. "You do seem quite protective of her."

"I'm all she has."

"I think she may need more, Jordan."

Her statement didn't surprise him. He wasn't blind to the happenings around him, and Jess had proven herself to be one who spoke her mind. "If you're referring to her developing disability, she has standing appointments with several professionals in the city. She's seen everyone from doctors to counselors to speech pathologists. She's getting the utmost care to deal with this as it happens."

Jess looked down. "That's not what I'm referring to. I figured you would have that part handled given what I know of you already."

"You say that like it's a bad thing almost."

She shrugged. "No, it's not. But sometimes matters require more than the writing of a check."

"Like what?"

"When I think of what you've told me about her. All she's been through in the past couple of years..."

What exactly was she getting at? "Not to sound harsh, but what exactly is your point? I'm getting her the best care that money can buy."

Jess let out another long breath. "Exactly. Maybe what she needs isn't something that can be bought."

Jess tucked a strand of hair behind her ear. Her hand seemed to be trembling ever so slightly as she spoke again. "She lost her father, a somewhat stable home. After she watched him get ill. Then her mother abandoned her."

"I told you she's in the care of a child counselor."

"I'll try again. Look around you, Jordan. Look at this island. This community. There has to be a reason this is the place you chose."

He shrugged. "Of course there is. My mother had wonderful stories about growing up here. We even visited a few times when I was a child. I know what a tight-knit community this is."

She clasped her hands in front of her chest. "Yes. Bingo. It is a tight-knit community. And the sooner she gets the sense of belonging and welcome that I'm sure this town is ready to greet you both with, well, I think it would do a world of good."

"Maybe you should just come out and say what you're leading to, Jess."

She literally braced both hands on the counter in front of her. Whatever she was about to tell him had her grasping for support.

"I want Sonya to feel like she belongs here.

That she can make friends here and find an extended family. She's reaching for a connection, Jordan."

Like you did when you moved here, he thought but kept the thought to himself.

"How do you propose that happens?"

"Well, I know we touched upon it briefly already. And I hope it's not too presumptuous of me to bring it up again."

Jordan had a small inkling of where this might be heading. He simply waited for her to continue.

"I think it would be a good idea to let her start by participating in the community center play."

By the time Jess made it home, all she wanted was a hot, steamy shower. But her phone started blowing up as soon as she powered it back on. Mostly texts from Clara.

I'm dying to hear how your evening went with you-know-who.

There were four other follow-up texts along the same theme. Also a voice mail from Travis. She couldn't bring herself to quite listen to that just yet. As much as she adored Travis, she would never see him as anything more than Kelly's older sibling. And her older brother by extension. He'd been subtle and not so subtle over the years about his desire to develop something more between them. And for the most part, he'd accepted the circumstances. Still, she didn't want things to be awkward between them like they had been last evening when she and Jordan had run into him.

Jordan. How she wished she could read him better. To his credit, he hadn't overreacted at her mention of the *Mother Goose* play. Part of her feared he might. He just reiterated why he was against the idea and that he was too tired to get into the matter right then. And that his spreadsheet still needed some work.

In other words, he'd effectively dismissed her when she'd brought up the topic.

Well, she'd done what she could. If she got the chance, she would try again. For Sonya's sake.

But for now she had to try and get all thoughts of Jordan Paydan out of her head. Easier said than done, she thought and peeled off her clothing to jump into the shower finally.

Her phone was still pinging with messages by the time she got out. Muttering under her breath about nosy coworkers, she went to mute it once and for all. As much as she loved Clara, she was in no mood to discuss all that had transpired between her and Jordan.

But the latest message wasn't from her boss. It was from the man himself. And his message indeed took her by surprise.

Please let me know date and time of next rehearsal. Sonya will be there. J

All in all, the performance could be considered a success, Jess thought as she stood onstage with her cast of children three weeks later. Only one major piece of scenery had toppled over and only half the children had flubbed their few lines. Granted, the other half had completely forgotten theirs. Jess was just glad it was all over as she took her bow along with her tiny castmates. They were receiving a standing ovation. Her gaze was drawn to the little girl standing at the other end of the stage with a wide grin on her face as she bowed before the applause.

Sonya had been a natural. She only had three very short lines but so did most of the other children. And she'd delivered them beautifully. The little girl had not missed one rehearsal in the three weeks since her brother had surprised Jess by giving her the go-ahead. Her assumptions about Sonya being included had been spot-on, if she did say so herself. The other children had immediately embraced Sonya as one of their own. If Jordan appreciated her role in his sister's newfound group of friends, he hadn't bothered to acknowledge it. In fact, she hadn't seen him much at all over these past three weeks, only in passing. Sonya had been dropped off and picked up for each session by her nanny. Never him. Just as well, Jess figured. She needed time to try and curb her growing attraction to a man who was so utterly wrong for her. Jordan was high society, New York City elite. She was a completely different breed. He'd always be the jet-setting city man while she had finally found a stable comfortable existence on a coastal island.

She'd thought that she could overcome such differences with Gary, and look how that had turned out.

Only, the plan to try and forget about Jordan hadn't quite worked. She'd thought about him constantly since having coffee that morning in his kitchen.

Either he was avoiding her, or she'd made much more of their activities at Kimby's than he apparently had. Jess hmmphed under her breath as the children scrambled off the stage and ran toward their parents. What did it matter if Jordan appreciated her suggestion or not. She hadn't done it for him. She'd done it for his sister.

He had to be out there. There was no way he would have missed Sonya perform.

"Don't forget," she called to them before they got far. "After-party on South Beach. Your parents all know where to go."

Maybe Jordan would even show up for that gathering. She couldn't deny that she hoped he would. That she wanted to see him again. Nor could she deny that a day hadn't gone by when she hadn't thought about him and what he might be doing. While he'd probably forgotten who she was.

Why else would he be so completely MIA?

It didn't matter. She refused to look for him in the audience. Her pride wouldn't allow it. But her eyes had other ideas. She spotted him a few rows back from the center of the stage. He leaned forward to give his sister a hug with one arm and pulled a colorful bouquet of flowers from behind his back with the other. He handed them to her. The child's delight was nearly palpable though she stood half an auditorium away.

The image took her breath away. Even from a distance she felt a pang of longing for him that no other man had ever evoked within her. He wore a black collared T-shirt with fitted khakis that flattered his trim and muscular physique. Despite the casual wear, he looked every bit the international tycoon that he was. A tycoon who had made sure to make time for his little sister's performance of a swan in *Mother Goose.* Jess forced herself to look away. There was no time to stand here and wallow in her longing. About three dozen guests were headed toward the beach now where some of her colleagues were already setting up.

And if one of those guests happened to be Jordan Paydan, well, she'd just have to pretend he was no different than any of the other parents.

She made those words a mantra as she drove

toward the coast and greeted the parents as they arrived. No sign of Jordan. Doubtless this little beachside party of hers to celebrate her hard work and that of the children was too lowbrow for him. He was probably taking his sister and Elise to a fancy gourmet restaurant to celebrate instead. His loss, she thought with no small degree of petulance. Her party was a huge success. With an impressive showing, good music and a variety of food between all her cooking and the various potluck dishes her guests so graciously provided.

But her heart did a little flip in her chest when she heard his voice from behind as she refilled the ice bucket.

"You sure know how to throw a hopping soirée."

Jess made sure to compose herself before she turned to face him. *No different than any of the other parents...*

"Welcome, Jordan. Glad you made it."

Elise and Sonya stood a few feet away, the nanny chatting with one of the other moms.

"We wouldn't have missed it," Jordan said.

"Thank you." She had to resist the urge to roll her eyes. That was the best response she could come up with? Another of those unbearable awkward silences ensued between them. All the times she'd rehearsed in her head the conversations they would have once she finally saw him again, and all she'd managed to come up with was a lame, "Thank you."

"Can I get you something to drink?" she asked by way of recovery.

Only that made no sense either, as he was already holding a sweaty bottle of beer. Why was it so hard to know what to say to this man?

He chuckled as he held it up. "All set. And I'm the one who should be thanking you."

Jess tried to feign nonchalance.

"Really?"

"Definitely. And also admitting that you were right. From the very beginning. Being a part of this production has done a world of good for Sonya. She's been upbeat and bouncy for the past three weeks. Since she started attending rehearsals with you. Even had a couple of playdates over. I believe that's what they're called these days?" He turned to glance in the direction his little sister stood blowing fat soap bubbles with two other girls. "And she seems less focused on her hearing loss. Is even attempting to speak more. Though we still have a long way to go."

"I'm so glad to hear all that, Jordan. Thank you for saying so."

"It's all your doing, Ms. Raffi."

She shook her head in argument. "No. Sonya just needed a springboard. I'm just glad I was able to help her find one."

He took a swig of his beverage and turned back to focus on her. "I wanted to ask you about something actually, to maybe see about maintaining her momentum."

"I'll help any way I can."

"She's already signed up for those swim classes at the center. I wanted to see about her taking your art class, as well."

It would have been a terrific idea. If only he'd asked a couple of weeks ago. "I'm afraid my class has ended, Jordan. I only have one session in the summer. There isn't enough interest once the season really kicks into gear. The children don't want to be cooped up in a room indoors on hot days when they could be cooling off on the beach or at a pool."

Jordan's expression clouded with disappointment. "I see. Makes sense." He uttered a small curse under his breath. "Looks like I blew it. Again." He seemed to have added the last word almost on a whim.

"Maybe I could stop by once in a while? Show her some basic techniques."

He broke into a wide smile. "You would do that?"

"Of course. It'd be my pleasure. I have plenty of time now that I won't be teaching again until the fall."

He rubbed his chin. "Then why don't we make it a regular thing?"

"Regular?"

"Yes. You could be a tutor of sorts. Maybe once or twice a week." He took a swig of his beer before continuing. "Who knows? The arrangement might do wonders for Sonya. It might even serve as a therapeutic outlet. One of the specialists we consulted mentioned art therapy as something we should consider."

Jess held her hands up to ward off the idea before he went any further with it. "Whoa. I need to be clear. By no means am I licensed or qualified as an art therapist."

He shrugged. "I understand that."

"I'd simply be spending some time with her. Showing her how to paint."

"I understand that, too. But it could be a start. It would at least give us an idea about whether Sonya might find it helpful."

Jess chewed the inside of her lip. On the surface, Jordan's proposal seemed like a reasonable suggestion. Only something about the whole scenario didn't sit right, made her uneasy. But she'd be doing it for Sonya.

"Of course, I'd be paying you for your time," Jordan added.

There it was again. Jordan was so ready to throw money at an issue in order to address it.

"I refuse to be paid for this, Jordan."

"But—"

She cut him off. "I mean it. There will be no money involved."

Her resolve must have sounded clear in her voice for Jordan didn't bother to argue, he simply gave her a small nod. "All right. When can you start?"

CHAPTER SEVEN

JESS BLEW OUT a breath of exasperation before she could answer Jordan's question. Somehow, she'd just agreed to regularly visit Jordan Paydan's home to provide artistic lessons to his little sister. How in the world had that happened?

"I can't start until next week," she finally answered. "I'm heading out of town this Friday."

He quirked an eyebrow in question. "Oh? An exciting trip planned?"

If only. No, the reason for her absence was not one she was looking forward to. "Something like that," she answered. "In fact, I'll be heading into your old home city. Manhattan, to be precise. There's an event I'm expected at."

"An event?"

She nodded. "An awards ceremony. My mother is due to receive an industry award. But she's out of the country still. I've been asked to go retrieve it for her at their annual dinner."

"Sounds prestigious."

"Oh, yes. It was emphasized to me repeatedly exactly how prestigious it is. I don't dare dream of missing the honor in her place."

She hadn't meant to sound so put out. But Jordan's reply confirmed that she had indeed. "You don't sound like you're looking forward to it in any way."

"Sorry. It's just that I don't really travel in those circles and it's hard when you don't know anyone. I'm just going to show up, have a meal, grab the little statuette when it's handed to me. And then come back home."

The look Jordan gave her was one of a man who'd just gotten an inspired idea. She could almost see the proverbial lightbulb above his head. That thought nearly had her giggling, even though her head was spinning from the latest development that had her instructing Sonya at his house.

What in the world was he getting at now?

"What is it?" she asked.

"Maybe you don't have to attend the dinner alone." He stepped closer to her and she got another whiff of the now oh-so-familiar aftershave that sent her senses soaring.

"I don't follow."

"You aren't going to believe this but I'm due in the city myself this weekend. For a charity auction and banquet. On Saturday evening. It's being held in honor of the American Auditory Association. They fund several research projects around the world to advance hearing and auditory causes. I normally don't like to attend such things but given the cause…"

What did any of that have to do with her? "And?"

"And I hate attending such events alone also. But I haven't had time to think too much about a plus-one given the move and everything else. Maybe we can assist each other?"

"I see." It was all she could stammer out. If she was hearing him correctly, he was asking her to accompany him to a charity gala. And offering to accompany her to the awards dinner in return. Somehow, in the span of one conversation, her life was becoming more and more intertwined with that of Jordan Paydan's, between her agreeing to instruct Sonya and now this potential trip.

But maybe she was looking too deeply into it. After all, she'd simply agreed to teach art to a child in her free time. And going to New York with Jordan wasn't all that different a prospect than how she'd shown him around Bimby's the other day.

Again, on the surface of it, Jordan was simply making a very reasonable suggestion and offer to accompany her. Generous even. On the surface, she'd be a fool to turn him down.

It was a crazy idea. Of course it was. He shouldn't have even brought it up. But they were both mature adults. Plus, the travel together would even give them some time to discuss Sonya and any benefits she might get from learning a new craft from Jess. And hadn't he already proven that he could stay away from her when he wanted to?

Not that he'd actually *wanted* to avoid her. Just some simple self-preservation.

It was clear Jess was dreading going to this awards ceremony by herself. There was no reason she had to. Not when he'd literally be in the same city at the same time.

Besides, he owed her for what she'd done for Sonya with the play. His little sister had been more engaged and upbeat than he'd ever seen her in the past couple of years. There was no denying the role Jess played in her transformation. And now she'd be instructing the little girl and refused to even be paid for it.

"So, a quid pro quo?" she asked.

"Something like that. We can suffer through our respective events together."

She chewed the inside of her cheek as she turned it over. "I suppose it makes sense."

"It's more a business proposition, really. We'll be helping each other with our individual transactions."

She finally looked up to face him. "Why not?"

Not the most enthusiastic of acceptances but what did he expect? It wasn't as if he was proposing a romantic getaway. Like he'd just told her, simply business.

"It's a plan, then. I'll have my assistant relay you the details."

"Okay. I'd planned on checking into my hotel early Friday morning. Maybe we can meet up later that day."

"Jess. You're not going to need a hotel. I have an apartment on the Upper East Side. There's plenty of room."

That drew her back a step. "Unless you're uncomfortable with that for some reason."

"Uh… No. Why would I be?"

Why indeed? "Well, I assure you there's enough space that we probably won't even run into each other."

"Good to know. Maybe we should draw up a contract and have it notarized."

He blinked at her. "I beg your pardon?"

"Never mind. Lame attempt at a joke." A laughing child squealed by, nearly colliding with Jess, and he didn't get a chance to further inquire what she'd meant.

"If you'll excuse me, I should tend to some of the other guests."

Okay. He stepped aside. "Of course, I didn't mean to dominate all of your time."

She gave him a tight smile and walked away.

Had he insulted her somehow? For the life of him he couldn't imagine how. Jordan took another swig of his beer and watched her back. Dressed in a cherry-red sundress with delicate swirly yellow patterns, she looked every bit the attentive elementary teacher. The one most of the boy pupils had a crush on. Definitely much sexier than any instructor he'd ever had. The dress cinched at her narrow waist, its skirt falling just above the knees. Very appropriate, very proper. So why couldn't he stop imagining taking it off her?

Perhaps he would never really understand this woman or the way he reacted around her.

It was a mere business transaction he was offering. His assistant had to send her the details. They wouldn't even have to run into each other aside from their respective events.

Jess blew a strand of hair off her forehead as she thought of the way Jordan had made his "proposition," as he'd called it. He wasn't even pretending he actually wanted to spend time with her. She should have told him no. That she'd rather go into the city alone. But that would have been a lie. As staid and cold as Jordan made his offer sound, the truth was she would rather attend the banquet accompanied by another person. To have that person be someone as charming and handsome as Jordan was just icing on the cake.

As far as spending the weekend in his New York City apartment, that would require some consideration. She wasn't sure she was ready for that. Who was she kidding? It was more accurate to say she wasn't sure she could handle it. Knowing he was so close, right within the same living space. With no one else there but the two of them.

She stole a glance at him as he chatted with some of the other parents. Correction—not parents. More specifically, he was surrounded by several of the moms. Each one of them seemed to be hanging on his every word whenever he spoke. He certainly had their full focus. He seemed natural and at ease in the group. Clearly, Jordan was used to female attention.

Before she could look away, he looked up and caught her eye. Great. He just had to catch her watching him.

A small tug at the hem of her skirt pulled her attention. One of her students, a little boy named Markey.

"Ms. Raffi. Would you dance with me?" He pointed over to the center of the yard where several of the children and a couple of adults had formed a makeshift dance floor and were doing a very silly rendition of the Chicken Dance to a bouncy hip-hop number.

"Why I'd be honored." She answered the child with an exaggerated mock bow then took his hand to lead him to the group of revelers.

The music changed after a few moments and the dancers switched to the Electric Slide. To her surprise, from the corner of her eye, she saw Jordan join in the dance with his little sister. She could guess whose idea that had been. Sonya was really making large strides toward breaking out of her shell.

Her partner noticed them, too. Markey squealed when he saw his little friend and ran over to Sonya, leaving her standing there doing the Electric Slide by herself. With a laugh, Jess made a move to walk away. But a wall in the form of pure, hard muscle suddenly appeared in her vision.

"Looks like we both lost our dance partners," Jordan said with a playful wink.

"I guess so. Little boys can be so fickle."

Jordan bent at the waist in a mock bow. "May I have the honor of taking over for Mr. Markey?"

Jess had to laugh at his playful tone. "It would be my pleasure, Mr. Paydan. What would be your preference this evening? The Chicken Dance perhaps? Or maybe the Twist?"

"Uh. Neither?"

"Ah, free-form, then. I like the lack of structure."

He threw back his head with a loud bark of laughter. "And people say I'm too rigid and unyielding."

"Not on the dance floor, it would seem."

To her surprise, Jordan was a competent dancer. Despite the silly soundtrack—kiddie versions of modern pop songs, he was able to move in tune with the music.

"I'm impressed," she told him.

One of the children had obviously gotten a hold of her outdoor speaker because the music suddenly grew much louder. "I'm a man of many talents," he said over the noise.

Jess couldn't argue the point. Too bad she couldn't feel as distant about him as he so obviously did about her.

How had she ended up here? Jess had to wonder as she stared out over the breathtaking view of the Manhattan skyline through the wall-to-wall window of Jordan's penthouse apartment. Somehow, she'd agreed to all of it—being delivered to his building in the car service he had sent for her, attending two gala events as his companion, canceling her original hotel reservations. Oh, and there was also that whole thing about spending two nights in the apartment of a man she barely knew and one she couldn't really control her emotions around.

Even from up this high, the hustle and bustle of the city was almost palpable from the streets below. She could see Central Park in the distance. The day was a clear and sunny one. Perfect for exploring one of the most dynamic cities in the world. Too bad she would have to do so alone.

"You made it. I thought I heard you." She heard Jordan's voice behind her.

He appeared to be business casual this afternoon. Black suit trousers and a smooth, crisp white button-down shirt with the collar undone. Though he appeared every bit the successful businessman back home on Martha's Vineyard, it was blatantly obvious that here in the city he was truly in his element. How in the world would someone like Jordan be happy long-term on a small island? Even one as cosmopolitan as Martha's Vineyard?

He looked so devilishly handsome she wanted to grab a sketch pad and draw his portrait.

"Yes, your housekeeping service let me in just as they were leaving. I hope that's okay."

"Of course."

"This is quite the view. I'm impressed."

He came to stand beside her and she got a hint of that subtle aftershave. His scent had somehow become both familiar and exotic to her senses.

"I've lived in this apartment for close to four years and that view still takes my breath away every time I see it."

It was clear in his voice how much he missed this place. And he'd given it all up. To move to New England, of all places.

"You must miss it," she ventured, to see if he would take the opening to discuss the motivation that made him move.

At his rather long pause of silence, she prodded further, her curiosity winning out. "You never mentioned what made you leave the city exactly."

"I decided we needed a quieter, more peaceful setting after…"

"After what?"

Jordan closed his eyes, released a deep sigh.

"Sonya was involved in a car accident. Shortly after she became my responsibility."

Jess gasped at the revelation. "Oh, Jordan. I'm so sorry. She seems to have recovered well."

"So the doctors tell me."

He clearly didn't believe them. Not completely. "Do you have some doubt that there might be lingering effects?"

"I don't know," he said simply, flatly. "But I did know I had to get her away from the crazy hustle and bustle of Manhattan. To someplace quieter. Like the vineyard."

Every etch of anguish on his face made it clear that Jordan blamed himself for what had happened to his little sister. Had he somehow caused the accident? As much as she wanted to press for details, she had to let him take the lead on this. But would he want to?

His next words answered her silent question and proved he wasn't ready to do so. "What about you?" he asked, effectively changing the topic back to her. She would let him, if it meant distracting him from the clear pain she saw on his face.

"You said you studied in Boston," he added.

"That's right."

"So how'd you end up settling down in Martha's Vineyard? You originally followed your college roommate but ended up staying even though she'd left."

The familiar feelings of hurt and anger washed over her though she tried hard to fight them. Even though five years had passed, the final argument with Gary still served as a cutting memory.

"There really was nowhere else to go." Jess couldn't help the hitch in her voice as she said the words. "Staying in Boston wasn't an option."

"Why's that? It's a great city."

"My leaving wasn't about the city." *It was about a boy*, she added under her breath.

Jordan was astute enough to figure out the gist of things. "A man out there was foolish enough to let you go?"

Jess tried not to gasp out loud at his bold statement. She should tell him not to say such things. For she had no way to interpret them. For all she knew, Jordan was simply offering empty words to make her feel better.

"One could argue that I was the one who was foolish." She continued to stare at the scenery before her, trying to gather her thoughts before continuing. "For not realizing sooner that it wasn't me he wanted. Not really. It was a certain version of me, the one he was originally introduced to. The one I didn't want to be anymore."

Curse her artist's mind for holding on to the most minute of details. She could clearly still see the utter disdain on Gary's face when she'd made the announcement that she was leaving graduate school to pursue teaching art. He couldn't grasp that she'd made the decision in order to avoid the slow death of her soul. After all, enrolling in business school had never actually been about *her*. Gary wasn't interested in hearing about any of that. He wanted his future wife to be someone on the fast track, with a high-profile career in the business world. He had no use for a struggling artist still looking to find her way. He hadn't even pretended otherwise for even the slightest moment when she'd told him.

"Like I said, he must have been a fool," Jordan declared. Before Jess could come up with a response, he turned to her abruptly. "Let's leave all that for now. Can I get you anything?

Some coffee? Or I daresay you could use a glass of wine," he asked, changing the subject altogether. Which was fine with her.

She shook her head. "Definite no to the wine. I'm not one to start imbibing this early."

He gave her a smile that almost had her knees buckling. Oh, dear. Perhaps this hadn't been such a great idea, after all. Her hotel would not have compared to the luxury of this apartment and had no chance of offering such a majestic view of the skyline. But it certainly would have been safer.

"Are you sure?" he asked. "It occurs to me that you should treat this as a mini holiday of sorts. You mentioned you hadn't been off the island to travel since permanently moving there. And I think you could use a vacation after putting a performance of *Mother Goose* on with a group of elementary children."

She chuckled softly. "It did take a bit of work."

"And a wealth of patience, I'm sure. You're a saint for not having lost it more than once."

"Not that much of a saint. I did come close."

"Then it's settled. We'll have to work to make

this as relaxing and as much of a getaway for you as possible."

"We? I thought you said that you had plenty to do and that we might not even come across each other aside from the parties."

He shoved his hands in his pockets and ducked his head slightly "About that. Due to some unforeseen developments, my latest deal has gone much smoother than anticipated. I find myself with some unexpected free time. A rarity for me."

Jess's heart pounded in her chest at where he might be leading with all this. "You do?"

"Yes. And now that I'm back home in New York, it occurs to me how much I've missed it. All the places I used to frequent, the mere atmosphere of Manhattan."

Jess waited for him to continue, not daring to interrupt.

"I'd like to show you some of it, if you're up for it," he added.

Was she hearing him correctly? Jordan actually wanted to spend time with her to show her around New York?

She tried to temper her response. It wouldn't do to sound too anxious or excited. Nothing in Jordan's suggestion sounded anything more than two near-friends taking advantage of some free time in a fun city. And it would serve her to not read anything more into it than that.

Still, she couldn't help but feel somewhat giddy. Jordan had to know countless people here where he'd grown up. She had no doubt there was more than one woman who wouldn't waste any time in showing up at the front door of his building if he called with any type of invitation.

"I think that would be lovely, Jordan."

He flashed another smile at her, even more effecting than the last one. "Great. We can start with lunch. Unless you've eaten already?"

The car service from the mainland he'd provided her with had come equipped with a beverage bar and a cooler case full of snacks. Jess had allowed herself to indulge in a bit of the finer gourmet chocolate. The ride had been quite long, after all. Probably the smoothest, richest chocolate she'd ever had, made from the finest cocoa. So she wasn't particularly hungry. But this wasn't an offer she was going to turn down.

"A girl's gotta eat lunch," she replied.

* * *

"Since both our respective soirées include dinner, I insist on treating for lunch," Jess declared as they stepped off the elevator and into the lobby of Jordan's high-rise building. And what a grand lobby it was. Even the most luxurious hotels she'd stayed at, and there hadn't been that many, didn't really compare to the grandeur of this entryway. A huge cement flowerpot filled with exotic, colorful branches sat atop a marble stand in the center of the area. Heavy burgundy curtains hung from immensely tall windows off either side. Elaborate, decorative artwork adorned the ceiling.

A fully uniformed attendant held the glass door open for them.

"So nice to see you again, Mr. Paydan."

Jordan gave the man a nod and a wave as they exited.

"That's not necessary, Jess," Jordan said in response to her offer as they began to walk. "You're here as my guest. Lunch is on me."

He was only half right. "And you're to be mine in return. I insist on lunch being my treat."

Jordan shrugged. "So be it."

Jess released a sigh of relief that he wasn't

going to argue. She wanted to contribute at least a little given everything Jordan was providing for this trip. But then a nagging twinge of apprehension blossomed in her chest. What if the place Jordan had in mind to eat was woefully out of her league? And her budget?

A distinct possibility. She looked around their surroundings. A bright red, foreign-looking sports car rolled smoothly down the road next to them. An older woman in a crisp navy suit and impossibly high-heeled stilettoes walked by with a tiny Pomeranian in her handbag. Even for Manhattan, they seemed to be in a particularly swanky part of town. She looked down at her faded jean leggings and scuffed-up tennis shoes. Why hadn't she thought to pack something nicer? Unlike her, Jordan, of course, seemed to fit right in.

Well, she couldn't back out of her offer now. Her pride wouldn't let her. Her one major credit card was an option. Though it was perilously close to the limit. She'd spent way too much on art supplies for her classroom at the beginning of the session. The center didn't provide much in the way of materials. Not for all the projects she liked to have her students create.

Plus, she always tended to go a bit overboard when buying paints and brushes.

Jordan was making small talk about all sorts of New York spots but she was too wound up to listen.

Her mind conjured up the worst-case scenario—she would sink right into the floor in humiliation if the restaurant declined her card in front of Jordan. Maybe she could sneak into the back and offer to come back later and wash dishes.

She was so preoccupied and nervous about that prospect that it came as a bit of a startle when Jordan suddenly stopped. They'd walked much farther than she realized. In fact, the area she found herself in seemed completely different than the first couple of blocks past Jordan's building.

"Earth to Jess." Jordan waved a hand over her face. "We're here. This is the place I had in mind for lunch."

A diner. They were entering the doors of an old-fashioned fifties diner complete with a wraparound counter and padded seat booths. A near giddy sense of relief washed over her as they found a table. Her bank account could definitely handle a diner meal even in this metropolis.

A waitress walked by balancing a pot of coffee and a plate that held a massive tower of a sandwich. "Be right with you, sweeties," she declared with a snap of her gum.

"Oh, dear. Are all the menu options that colossal?"

Jordan winked at her. Such a small, meaningless thing but her stomach quaked at the playfulness. He really did seem to be a completely different person here. Not to make excuses for him, but the idea had to explain at least partly why he'd been just so downright grumpy when she'd first laid eyes on him while painting Sonya's wall. He'd probably begun missing his true home already.

"Only the ones worth getting," he answered her question.

The waitress plopped two plastic-encased thick menus in front of them. Her name tag said "Rona" in cursive lettering. She pointed at Jordan. "I thought that was you. Where ya been lately, sugar?"

"I'm only in the city part-time for the foreseeable future."

Rona snapped her gum once more. “Huh. Well, we missed ya around here.”

“And I missed this place.” There was no doubting the sincerity of his words. Jess got the impression he was speaking of more than just the diner. Whatever had happened to Sonya last year, Jordan had disrupted his entire life in response.

“Then don’t be a stranger when you’re back, doll.”

She turned to Jess. “What can I get ya?”

After they’d each ordered and Rona walked away, Jess studied Jordan from across the table. He’d leaned against the back of the booth and stretched his arms across the top, more relaxed than she’d ever seen him. His shirt appeared molded to his broad, muscular chest. If possible, he looked even more handsome. As if he was more relaxed and it added to his striking good looks.

“What is it?” he asked in response to her scrutiny.

“Nothing. Just that…” Jess hesitated. She didn’t want to impose on his lighthearted mood in any way.

But then he prompted her further. “Go ahead, Jess. Penny for your thoughts.”

“It’s just, you seem really happy to be back.”

She’d been right. His jaw suddenly grew tight and he glanced out the window with a sudden faraway look in his eyes.

“You’re very observant. I am glad to be back in New York.”

She wasn’t expecting the words that followed.

“And I’m really glad you’re here with me to share it.”

CHAPTER EIGHT

HE HADN'T EXPECTED to say that last part out loud. The way Jess's eyes grew wide with surprise and how she'd ducked her head afterward was confirmation that he shouldn't have.

But it was so easy to let his guard down around her. And she could clearly read him well. She was right. He was happier to be back in New York than he'd imagined. He was growing fonder of his new home by the day, but that was different. It had yet to feel like home the way being here did.

"Thank you," she offered simply in reply.

He'd clearly made her uncomfortable. Why was that? Her response was certainly a rather tepid one. Maybe she didn't want to entertain the notion that he was regarding her as more than a weekend companion—because she didn't feel the same way.

He didn't need her to feel uncomfortable

around him. Or it was going to be a long forty-eight hours.

"It's always a pleasure to show someone new around my hometown city," he quickly added.

See, Jess. Nothing more than two near-friends enjoying a couple of days playing tourist and guide.

Never mind that the thought sent a flow of disappointment through his center. He wasn't going to read into things or speculate about feelings that weren't there. Based on their conversation back at his penthouse, she was clearly nursing her wounds from a relationship gone sour. And heaven knew he didn't have it in him to pursue any kind of real relationship. He had to make things right with Sonya first. Make sure she was adjusted and settled into her new life and reality.

No, he didn't have much to offer at the moment. And a woman like Jess deserved more than he was ready to give of himself.

He'd never in his life pushed for anything from a woman. Certainly not for friendship. And definitely not for anything more. He wasn't about to start with Jess Raffi. Even if he had spent most of the morning imagining all the popular spots he could take her to and what her reaction might be to various places he typically took for granted as a native New Yorker. He'd be hard-pressed to explain exactly why he was looking forward to it so much. If someone had told him two weeks ago that he'd welcome the prospect of playing tour guide to a first-time visitor, he would have laughed out loud.

Though he couldn't deny how easy it was to spend time with her, how comfortable he felt around her. There was no denying the tension in the air between them. But above that there was a sense of familiarity and warmth he hadn't yet experienced with another woman.

Or anyone else, for that matter.

"So you never told me exactly what this award is your mother is getting," he ventured as the waitress dropped off their orders.

Given what he knew about Jess and her giving nature, he presumed her mother must be up for some type of humanitarian honor. And that a renowned magazine had sponsored the charity. The apple and tree and all that. He definitely hadn't been expecting the reason Jess gave him.

"A photo spread she did last year for *Geo-*

graphic World magazine garnered a lot of praise and attention. They're granting her their excellence in photo journalism award."

Jordan stilled in the act of salting his fries. "Your mother is a photographer for *Geographic World* magazine?"

She nodded and popped an olive into her mouth. "That along with some other publications and websites. It made for an interesting childhood."

"I had no idea."

"Well, why would you? It hasn't exactly come up, has it?"

Because she'd never brought it up, Jordan thought. Even when she'd been telling him about the award gala. There had to be some kind of reason for that. Though he couldn't venture to guess.

"Your mom sounds like she leads quite a life."

"I suppose. Her job is more adventurous than it is glamorous. And it certainly doesn't pay as much as one would think. Especially considering the lifestyle she's had to lead."

He knew he wasn't imagining the hint of resentment in her voice. Probably something to do with that cryptic *interesting childhood* comment. It occurred to him just how little he knew about her. And just how badly he wanted to find out more. Everything, in fact.

"How?" he asked her.

"How what?"

"How did it make for an interesting childhood?"

A faraway look clouded over her eyes at the question. "Actually, *unconventional* might be a better word. It was great at first. Until it wasn't."

"How so?"

Jess didn't touch her food as she spoke. "My earliest memories are of traveling to these wonderful places and meeting the most wonderful people. Given her profession, my mother was quite the nomad. And I was nomadic with her for those early years."

"That changed, I take it."

"It sure did. Right at the time I turned twelve. She decided I could no longer travel with her then. That I needed a more steady education. And that it was hard enough for her to ensure her own safety and well-being while on the road less traveled. I had begun to attract more and more male attention in some of the more remote places we visited." She swallowed. "Her heart was in the right place, I guess."

"And after you turned twelve?"

"Constant change. My mom had quite an extended family. But no one really close. I was tossed from distant relative to distant relative as they would take me. Mostly throughout the Midwest."

Jordan let out a low whistle. "You're right. That is pretty unconventional. Right from the very beginning." No wonder she'd sought residence in a tight community.

"And what of your father? If you don't mind my asking."

She tried to hide her sudden flinch of pain, but it was hard to miss. "He wasn't in the picture much. You see, I'm a product of one of her adventures. She met a local man on one of her assignments. In Malaysia. A brief affair that led to… Well, that led to me." She spread her arms out wide.

Yeah, that certainly explained a lot. He'd wondered why a college graduate with her whole future ahead of her would stay in her roommate's hometown long after that roommate had moved away.

"My father stayed where he was and my mother simply moved on to the next assignment."

The same way she'd eventually moved on from her own daughter, Jordan thought. He couldn't resist the urge to reach across the table then and take her hand into his, half-afraid she would pull away.

She didn't.

Jess couldn't believe how much of her past she'd just shared—between their conversation at the penthouse earlier and all that she'd just divulged about herself. Something about Jordan loosened her tongue on topics she usually held close to her chest. Except for Kelly, no one had heard as much as she'd just confided in Jordan about her mostly absent parent.

Now as they walked out of the diner and down the street, she had to admit it had felt good to share some of her past with him. Like a bit of a release. Either Jordan Paydan had notable listening skills or she was growing closer to him than she wanted to admit. Hopefully, it was the former.

"I figured we could walk to Times Square,"

he told her. "After that meal, I for one could use the exercise or I'll need a nap before 3:00 p.m."

"I'd love to see Times Square."

He didn't break stride when he answered her. "You didn't think I was going to let you leave New York without visiting its most iconic tourist spot, did you?"

"I suppose that wouldn't do."

"Not at all."

Jordan turned the corner around the next building a little too swiftly with Jess fast on his heels. They nearly collided with a couple who were just standing there.

No. Correction. Jess realized they weren't simply standing still. A young man and woman were locked in a tight embrace, their lips fused in a passionate kiss.

"Um…excuse me," she uttered to the two strangers who clearly didn't hear her. They were much too engrossed with each other.

An awkwardness settled between them as they continued to walk. Jess couldn't resist taking a backward glance at the enamored couple. Such public displays weren't for everyone. Gary had certainly not been one to show any affection when others were present. But she had to wonder what it would be like, to be so consumed with passion for someone. So much so that the rest of the world simply ceased to exist, even on a crowded city sidewalk. She'd had her fair share of dates during her university days and in the period after her relationship had crumbled. After Kelly had gotten married, she'd been insistent on setting Jess up on more than a few blind dates with her new husband's friends. None of those men had sparked any kind of flame within her. The one brief relationship she'd had after moving to the island had left her wounded by rejection yet again. The man had completely ignored her once summer had ended and he'd gone back to his regular daily life. Her gaze shifted to Jordan's profile.

He might not technically be a tourist but he was no doubt cut from the same type of cloth. Despite his recent relocation, it was clear New York would always call to him. One day he would no doubt answer.

And what would that mean for her if she foolishly gave him her heart? Her summer fling had hurt after he'd left her high and dry without so much as a backward glance. But she'd hardly considered herself scarred afterward. The same could be said of her failed engagement to Gary. Something told her with Jordan the end result would be much more extreme. Far more devastating.

She studied him now. Jordan's chin was clenched tight, his hands jammed in his pockets. He had noticed the awkwardness, too, it appeared. Jess tried to come up with something to say, a witty retort that may help them to return to the easy camaraderie they'd seemed to share since eating at the diner. Nothing came to mind.

"Not much longer." Jordan finally spoke after they'd walked a couple of blocks. A few minutes later they reached the man-made wonder that was Times Square. Jess wasn't sure where to look first. So much was happening around her!

A news chyron scrolled across the building to her right. Neon billboards in every direction flashed advertisements for everything from cologne to skinny jeans to political messages. Music seemed to be sounding from every direction. A man wearing nothing more than tight

Speedo shorts and a straw hat played a string guitar a few feet away.

And there was a superhero approaching her wearing bright blue leggings and a long, flowing cape.

"Would the lady like a picture?" the masked man wanted to know.

She looked to Jordan in question but he was already pulling his cell phone out of his pocket. He motioned for her to stand next to the other man, then lifted his phone to focus the lens on the two of them.

After a few clicks, Jess stepped away. Jordan pulled a bill out of his wallet and handed it to the caped crusader. "Thank you, good citizen," he said before walking away.

Jess laughed as she watched the cape retreat. "Uh, what just happened?"

Jordan chuckled. "Simple. I just got a compelling picture to share with all your students back home."

"They're sure to be jealous."

He showed her the screen and flipped through the snaps he'd just taken. Jess's smile looked more like a grimace in every picture.

She groaned in consternation. "I'm usually

much more photogenic than that. I'm just not used to being snapped with caped strangers in the middle of a public square."

"I think you look lovely. Beautiful, actually."

But he wasn't looking at the screen as he said it. In fact, he'd turned to focus squarely on her face. Jess's stomach did a little flip. Suddenly, all the noise and commotion surrounding them faded into the background. Her focus narrowed completely on the man standing before her. Her mind went back to the couple they'd almost walked into on their way over here. Heaven help her, she wanted that. She wanted to feel what they felt as they held each other, locked in a passionate kiss.

And she wanted it with Jordan.

They were suddenly interrupted by a statuesque young lady in an elaborate lioness costume. She handed Jess a flyer before walking away. An advertisement for a Broadway play. Jess stared at it longingly. Jordan clearly noticed.

"You wanted to see a show?" he asked.

She shrugged, hoping to seem less than eager. "Doesn't everyone?"

Jordan gave her a smile that sent a curl of heat down to her toes. "Let's see what we can do."

Jordan wasn't going to give her a chance to protest as he called up his contact list on his screen and clicked on the number. He wished he'd thought of the idea himself. Of course, someone visiting this city for the first time would want to see a Broadway show. And if they saw a Saturday matinee, they would have plenty of time to get ready before the auction tomorrow evening. Jess didn't strike him as the type of woman who needed an exorbitant amount of time getting ready for events. And if she was, he got the impression he'd be forgiven considering what he was taking the time for.

She was looking at him expectedly when he disconnected the call. "It's all set."

"All set? Jordan, what did you just do?" She reached out to rest her hand on his forearm and he felt the warmth of her fingers as they touched his skin.

He shrugged. "I made a phone call to someone who owed me a bit of a favor. Simply collected."

"Someone who has access to show tickets, I presume."

"You got it. We are all set for a matinee showing tomorrow afternoon."

"Jordan, you didn't have to do that," she protested but the pleasure was clear in her voice and in her bright smile.

"You don't want to go, then?" He lifted his cell phone. "I can call back and cancel."

Her eyes grew wide with alarm and he had to chuckle. She gave him a useless shove. "You're teasing me."

She was right. And he was having an immensely pleasurable time doing so.

"Thank you, Jordan. I mean it." Jess was still expressing her gratitude half an hour later when they made it back to the lobby. Jordan had to wonder how often anyone had simply done something nice for her in her past.

"Don't thank me just yet. You may not like it."

She gave his arm a squeeze. "I know I'm going to absolutely love it."

Jordan called up the elevator and noticed

Jess resting a hand to her midsection. "Still full from lunch?" he asked with a laugh.

She returned his laughter. "Indeed. In fact, I might not even fit into the gown I plan to wear. It is rather formfitting."

He couldn't even help the images that sprang into his head—of Jess in a tight, silky dress. A strapless number that showed off her tanned olive skin and the bright honey color of her eyes. And then he pictured himself helping her out of it.

Enough.

"If you prefer a different outfit, there's a boutique on the ground floor, down the other hallway."

She studied her fingers. "I'm sure I wouldn't be able to afford a place like that. I don't typically shop at boutiques. Not with my part-time summer instructor job and the odd gig here and there."

Her words reminded him how much he sometimes took for granted. "You wouldn't have to pay for it, Jess."

She laughed at that. "Why is that? Does this boutique just give away dresses?"

He shrugged. "Let's just say I have some

credit there. And it isn't like I'll have the need to use it myself. It's a ladies' boutique. I'll call ahead and tell them to expect you."

She studied his face. "You're serious."

"Of course I am."

"Thank you. That's very generous. But that's not necessary. I'll wear one of the dresses I packed." Her tone suggested she would hear no argument. And he got the distinct impression he'd made her upset for some reason.

He certainly wasn't suggesting any type of charity. He did have an understanding with the manager who ran the store, an arrangement set up long ago for his mother while she was alive. His father had never bothered to change it and neither had he.

Jess appeared to want the topic closed for now. Though he couldn't guess why his suggestion would be upsetting in any way, he would respect her wishes.

"What color is it?" he asked, more to change the subject than any other reason. "Your dress."

"Why?"

"I should probably try and match my tuxedo sash or cuff links. Seeing as we're going together."

Her smile reappeared. "Have that many tuxedo accessories on hand, do you?"

Again, more reminders of all the little things he'd taken for granted in his life. Jess was doing more to point such things out than he'd encountered ever before. "I go to a lot of black tie events."

"Hmm. Sure sounds like it."

"It's hard to describe, actually. It's blue but more of a cross between sapphire blue and ocean blue with the most delicate gold detail spun over it. The material is silky but it isn't silk. Feels lighter than silk, believe it or not. It almost feels like liquid."

"Spoken like a true artist. Where in the world did you find such an exceptional item?"

She ducked her head. "My mother travels the world. Every once in a while, she'll see something and remember she has a daughter. I believe she picked this item up at the Grand Bazaar in Istanbul."

"I see."

Jordan wasn't surprised when she didn't take long to change the subject. "You know, some men might be envious."

He quirked an eyebrow at her. “About what, exactly?”

“All those extravagant parties you get to attend. With a line of beautiful women on your arm, no less.”

Jordan grunted at that. If she only knew. Most of those party invites were nothing more than networking opportunities or direct commitments he’d made to colleagues or friends. Often, he was tired and bored out of his mind, more than ready to be one of the first to leave. Much to the chagrin of some of his past dates.

So it surprised him just how much he was looking forward to the gala he’d be attending tonight. And that feeling had everything to do with the lady he’d be attending it with.

Jess had been right. There was no real adequate way to describe the dress she wore. Now as he watched her step out of her suite dressed for the award gala, Jordan felt as if the breath had been knocked out of him.

He’d found her beautiful and striking when he’d seen her in overalls back in Sonya’s room at the mansion. Dressed in an evening gown with her hair up, she was a vision out of some kind of fantasy.

How had she done all that in less than an hour? By herself, no less.

She gave him a shy smile as she approached. "What do you think?" she asked with a little twirl.

Think? Who could think at a time like this?

The dress may as well have been made specifically for her. The color brought out the reddish, copper highlights of her hair and accentuated the honey-gold specks of her bright hazel eyes. The fit fell somewhere between loose and formfitting with the light fabric hugging her body in all the right places. He'd never wanted to remove an article of clothing off a woman so badly in his life.

Her lips tightened at his continued silence, and a shroud of concern clouded her eyes. "Jordan, please tell me if you don't like it. You won't be offending me if you tell me the truth. Is it not formal enough? I've been worried about that."

He cleared his throat and forced his mouth to work. "It's perfect, Jess. Absolutely stunning."

And so was she.

* * *

She had to be in the middle of some kind of fairy tale. Jess sat in the backseat of the stretch limo, trying to process the moment she was living. A devilishly handsome man in a custom-tailored suit sat next to her as they drove through New York City in a chauffeur-driven limousine. When she'd first gotten the request to attend this ceremony in her mother's place, she'd never dreamed that she'd be arriving to it in such a fashion.

She'd fully expected to take a cab downtown from her low-key motel just outside the city—the only kind she could afford in this part of the state. Then she'd expected to walk in, sit at a table surrounded by a bunch of strangers and count the minutes till she could leave.

Instead, here she was, about to enter the ballroom on the arm of one of Manhattan's most eligible bachelors whose penthouse she was staying in. How could all of this be happening in one day?

Though she was trying hard not to think about why exactly a man like him would have a credit at a women's boutique. Only one explanation made sense. Jordan must entertain women often enough that he felt the need to secure a retail service on standby.

That prospect bothered her more than she cared to examine.

"Nervous?" Jordan asked next to her.

Yes. For all sorts of reasons. "Maybe a little. Particularly about the walking on stage part," she admitted.

He reached over across the seat and took her hand in his. Then he proceeded to brush the faintest of a kiss along her knuckles. Jess felt her insides turn to jelly. Heat swam through her core. Full-blown kisses from other men had evoked less of a response.

"You'll be fine," Jordan reassured her.

"Easy for you to say. You're quite accustomed to this kind of thing."

He chuckled. "I admit to having given a speech or two at various charity events."

"I'm sure you have. And that you were both charming and inspirational."

The strong, masculine hand around hers tightened ever so slightly. "Is that how you see me?"

The air suddenly grew heavy with his loaded question. How was she supposed to answer that?

Thankfully, Jordan spared her from having to. “Just focus on me and where I’m sitting. And think of how I’ll be silently cheering you on,” he added and gave her hand another squeeze.

As if she could focus on anything *but* him. The same way she had been pretty much since the first day they’d met.

“Thank you. That just may work.”

He didn’t let go of her hand and Jess was in no rush to do so, either. The contact was helping to reassure her in a way—about the award acceptance, that was. As far as her emotions regarding Jordan, his touch only seemed to be pushing those to the forefront and wreaking havoc on her equilibrium.

She didn’t feel any more steady when the car finally pulled up to the front of the banquet hall. On shaky legs, she let Jordan lead her out of the vehicle and up the stairs. A handful of photographers snapped a few photos as they entered the building but she was much too nervous to so much as smile, let alone stop to pose for pictures.

A well-heeled doorman in a dark suit met them at the ballroom doors and showed them to their table. The two couples already seated greeted them with warm smiles and brief introductions. Jess let out a sigh of relief as she settled into her chair. Wouldn't be long now before the whole thing was over. Only about two or so hours to go.

"I think you may need a drink," Jordan declared and motioned for a server.

"That might not be such a good idea. What if it goes to my head and I trip up the stairs?"

He laughed out loud at her potential embarrassment and she gave him a playful punch on the upper arm. "Then I shall gallantly come help you up and brush you off."

She hadn't expected to be quite this anxious. Jess cast a grateful glance in Jordan's direction where he sat next to her. Thank heavens he was here with her. He was truly a godsend or she'd be a quivering mess sitting here all by herself with the chair next to her remaining empty if it wasn't for him.

Jordan Paydan had certainly come through for her. When she hadn't even been aware that she'd been in need of rescuing.

CHAPTER NINE

"I HOPE YOU slept well," Jordan said as she stepped into the kitchen the next morning. Jess had awoken and immediately followed her nose to the origin of the smell of brewed coffee.

He was already dressed in gray pressed slacks and a crisp collared navy blue shirt. She looked down at her thick cotton socks and ragged sleepshirt with a cartoon depiction of a sleeping kitten on the front.

He handed her a steaming cup and any thought or care about her appearance fled. All she cared about right now was the caffeine.

"I slept great. Thanks." She really had. The award ceremony had taken a lot out of her last night. She'd fallen into slumber as soon as her head hit the pillow at half past midnight. "Are you headed out?" she asked, gesturing to his clothing.

He nodded. "There's a property over on Park

Avenue I've been meaning to look at, for a potential acquisition."

"No rest even on a Saturday morning for you, then?"

"I'm afraid not."

"So I have the morning to myself?" she asked with a bit too much enthusiasm.

Merriment filled his eyes. "Don't sound too disappointed." Amused sarcasm was clear in his voice.

Jess simply laughed in response. The truth was, she could use some time alone. Jordan's presence was wreaking havoc on her emotions. She needed some downtime to try and process it all. Maybe she'd find some paper and pens and do some sketching to help ground her. As it was, she was practically jumping out of her skin in anticipation of the theater show later this afternoon. She needed a distraction. Several sights from yesterday were etched in her mind, and her soul was crying out to get the images out in some type of physical form.

"I just wouldn't want to keep you from your work, is all," she replied.

Without responding, he glanced at his watch then set his mug down on the counter. "I'm going to get going. If you do want to head out, the car and driver are available. I can text you the number to call. Or there are shops on the first floor, as I mentioned yesterday."

Jess shook her head. "That won't be necessary. I'll enjoy the solitude."

"All right, then. I'll see you in just a couple of hours."

Jess gave him a small wave as he walked out then drained the rest of her coffee. She realized too late that she'd never asked him where he kept the paper and pens.

He had to have writing materials here. He was a businessman, after all. Jess doubted he'd mind if she used some. She wouldn't need much; she could work small.

She walked over to a mahogany writing table she'd noticed in her entry hall and pulled open the top drawer. There was indeed a writing pad and an elegant, silver ink pen sitting there in the center. But that was not what drew her eye. The drawer also held a three-by-five framed picture. Jess drew in a breath and picked it up.

He appeared to be not much older than ten or so when it had been taken. Jordan stood between an older gentleman who had to be his father and a breathtakingly lovely woman with an angelic smile. His mother. Jordan had her eyes and high cheekbones. They all looked so happy, so content to just be together. Jess rubbed her thumb over the image as it seared into her brain.

Jordan's apartment was very much like the mansion back on the island in that there were no photographs hung on any of the walls. In fact, the only photo she'd ever seen of Jordan outside of a gossip website was the one she held in her hand.

Jess had never considered herself to be particularly nosy. And she certainly hadn't meant to be snooping. But she couldn't tear her gaze away from the image in the frame. An uncomfortable feeling settled over her. She was clearly invading his privacy. If Jordan wanted this picture seen, he would have set it out on top of the desk.

It nagged at her that he'd hidden it. She could guess why. Jordan had had so much love in his early life. Only to have it all torn away. Of course, he had Sonya but that relationship came with an extraordinary amount of responsibility. And though countless women would be more than willing to share his life with him, the loss he'd endured was so clearly depicted in this one photograph.

Jess slowly put the frame back exactly in the spot it had been before pushing the drawer slowly shut. The pad and pen would have to stay there, too. She wouldn't want Jordan to realize she'd used them and hence seen the picture.

She'd drawn on paper towels before when inspiration had struck at odd times. She could do so again.

Their seats were even better than he'd expected. Jordan had no intention of telling her, but he told Jess a bit of a fib yesterday. He hadn't actually called in a favor. He'd instead gotten a hold of a friend with long-standing connections in the New York theater world and asked him for the best seats he could secure at such short notice. The friend had definitely come through. He and Jess had a dream spot with a clear view of the entire stage.

Sitting next to her now, Jess's excitement was almost palpable. He felt an odd thrill at being able to do that for her.

How many times had he been to a show and barely paid attention? There was always something on his mind—either a business matter or some other responsibility he was preoccupied with. But today's matinee felt different. Jess's enthusiasm about being here seemed to be rubbing off on him.

"The local theater productions I've attended don't quite compare to this venue," she said softly. Her eyes gazed around the auditorium, taking in every detail.

"It's all about scale, I guess."

"It's breathtaking."

Hopefully, she was about to enjoy an experience she'd remember for a good long while. He may have been to countless shows himself. But something told him this particular time would serve to provide him with rather a fond memory, as well.

"I wish the kids could see all this," Jess said on a sigh.

Why was he not surprised? Here she was about to experience something she'd always wanted to do, pulsing with excitement, and she was thinking of her pupils.

He'd never met anyone like her.

She continued, “Some of them were so into putting our little play together, quite the little thespians. Seeing all this would knock their socks off.”

He didn’t get a chance to respond as the lights started to flicker.

“It’s starting,” she said in a breathless whisper just as the lights began to dim and the musicians started to play. A tall, slim woman dressed completely in black began narrating the beginning of the story. When the curtain finally drew open, an auction scene started to play out on the stage.

Jess was literally sitting on the edge of her seat. Jordan realized he was paying as much attention to her reactions as he was to the drama unfolding onstage.

The scene ended and the lights dimmed once more but a chandelier between the stage and audience began to slowly light up. The orchestra started up again. Jordan knew what was about to happen. This was actually one of the plays he’d attended in the past, about four years ago, if he was remembering correctly. Jess was staring intently at the hanging chandelier. Suddenly, it dropped several feet before stopping about a dozen feet above their heads. The theatrical effect earned a collective gasp from the audience.

Jess jumped in her seat and let out a sharp cry. Then she clutched at his biceps. Her unexpected touch sent a jolt of electricity through his arm and straight into his chest. He didn't give himself a chance to overthink it, just placed his hand over hers and wrapped his fingers around her soft, smooth skin.

She didn't try to pull away. He wasn't sure he would have let her.

The sun had dimmed somewhat by the time they left the theater and stepped back outside. But it was still strong enough to cause a bit of a visual shock after sitting in the dark for close to two hours. Or maybe Jess's eyes were stinging as a result of the phenomena she'd just experienced. The drama, the music, the audience reactions. She'd enjoyed every minute of it.

"What'd you think?" Jordan asked her as they stepped outside the heavy glass doors along with the rest of the crowd.

"I don't have the words, Jordan."

Then she did the only thing she could think

of; she threw her arms around his neck in an embrace. It was simply meant to thank him. She'd truly been at a loss for the right words to do so. But the hug instantaneously turned to something else.

He responded by placing his hands around her waist, and then he pulled her closer. She could feel every inch of his hard, muscular length. The scent of him surrounded her; his warmth spread over her skin and through every cell in her body.

The only coherent thought that her mind could process was that he may kiss her. And how badly she wanted him to.

Was she brave enough to do anything about it? Out here, in the middle of this busy sidewalk, of all places?

Jess couldn't remember a time when she'd wanted something as badly as she wanted to feel Jordan's lips on hers, but she felt frozen with fear and doubt.

Whatever Jordan read in her eyes must have caused him to tighten his grip on her. His words made her wonder if he was somehow reading her mind.

"Jess, you have to tell me if this is what you

want," he said on a hoarse whisper, a hard edge grating his voice. "You have to say so if you want me to kiss you."

She couldn't make her mouth work.

Jordan went on. "Because if you say so, there'll be no turning back. I *will* kiss you. Maybe not here, not in front of all these people. But the first chance we're alone. It's going to happen. Your move. Your call."

An explosion of heat burst below her rib cage and moved fluidly lower. She wanted to tell him yes. That she wanted him to kiss her more than he would ever know.

There'll be no turning back.

Those five words encompassed the full strength of the emotions she felt at the moment. For he was right; there would be no turning back. Not for her anyway. Her heart would be forever changed.

The crowd around them grew larger and louder as more people exited their respective performances.

"Let's go." Without waiting for further response, Jordan took her by the hand and led her away.

Jess's heart pounded like a jackhammer in

her chest. She could barely hear the crowd over the roaring in her ears. "Wait. Jordan. Where are we going?"

"I could use a drink."

Jess couldn't decide whether she was relieved or disappointed. For a moment back there she'd thought maybe Jordan was about to lead her somewhere secluded. Somewhere that it would be just the two of them. Alone. And he could make good on the words he'd just whispered to her. But he'd made clear that any first move would have to come from her.

Was it wrong that a part of her wanted him to make the decision for her? To make the first move?

After all, she may never summon the courage to ask for what she so badly wanted. Because she would want so much more. More than Jordan could give at this moment in his life.

He was right. Perhaps they could both use a drink. But when he finally stopped pulling her along and opened the door to their destination, Jess realized they weren't in some kind of trendy, toney New York City bar.

Jordan had brought her to an ice cream counter. A large sign above the waitress stand said Best Milkshakes This Side of the Hudson.

A bubble of laughter escaped her lips. This man seemed to surprise her at every turn. She simply didn't know what to expect. It both exhilarated and terrified her.

"This is what you meant by a drink? A milkshake?"

He returned her laughter with a smile of his own. But the tightness in his face remained. She dared to hope it was because he was still thinking about kissing her.

"Not just any milkshake," he answered her. "The best milkshakes—"

"This side of the Hudson." She completed his sentence, pointing to the sign above their heads.

"I mean, it's no Bimby's," Jordan said as they selected a couple of seats at the front counter. "But that's a tough standard to beat."

"I'm glad to see you're acknowledging the correct hierarchy of our respective ice cream spots," she teased. The talk of Bimby's had her recalling the last time he had almost kissed her. In the artificial cave of the mini-golf attraction. She couldn't seem to get her mind off having Jordan's lips on hers.

"Don't bother looking at the menu." He interrupted her unwelcome thoughts. "You want the chocolate mocha."

Her stomach made a noise in protest. Between the excitement of the show and the thrill of having Jordan touching her, there was no way she was going to be able to consume something that rich and heavy. "I'm afraid I'm still full from lunch."

"All right. You can share mine."

The milkshake arrived with two fat paper straws sticking out of the tall sundae glass just as Jordan had requested. He pushed it toward her. "Ladies first."

She took a hesitant sip as he watched. There was something deliciously intimate about sharing a beverage out of the same glass. An explosion of coffee and chocolate filled her mouth. "Wow."

"What did I tell you?" he asked with a laugh.

"You weren't kidding. I'll admit, this place could give Bimby's a run for its money."

"Change your mind about wanting your own?"

She shook her head. "I'd better not."

The real truth was, she liked the idea of the

picture they must have made. As if they were a real couple, with their heads bowed over a single sundae glass. As if they'd been together for a while, intimate even. Two people in a solid relationship enjoying each other's company.

Is that the way they looked to the other customers sitting in this ice cream parlor? But there was an even bigger question that nagged at her.

Would she ever really have that with anyone? Least of all the man sitting next to her now?

Jess had no idea how badly Jordan wanted to crush his lips to hers. So he'd had to get them both away. Before he did something stupid in front of all those theatergoers. Like pull her to him and devour her mouth like he so badly wanted to do since he'd laid eyes on her this morning.

She'd looked right in his penthouse. Like she belonged there. With him.

He had to wonder how things would be between them if they'd just been two normal strangers who'd met under normal circumstances. Who knew? Maybe there was a small chance he would have met her even if he hadn't made the move to Martha's Vineyard. If his life was back to normal and he was a bachelor businessman without the responsibility of caring for a small child who was dealing with a developing disability. Maybe they might have even crossed paths while she was on this trip to accept her mom's award.

It was a fanciful notion, but he wanted to believe that he would have met Jess regardless of life events.

He sighed and watched her take another sip of the milkshake, those luscious, full lips tempting him even further. There was no use in speculating about what might have been. The reality was he *was* responsible for a child. He had to do everything in his power to make sure Sonya grew up healthy and happy. He'd messed that up once already with colossal results. He would never forgive himself if it were to happen again.

Heeding reality meant that he couldn't offer Jess the type of relationship a woman like her deserved from a man. Things like a full commitment, his full attention, his time.

He just didn't have any of it in him. Not now, not after the events of the year. Which made him oh-so-wrong for her. So he should have never asked her if she wanted him to kiss her. If he could take it back, he would. He would tell her how temporary this weekend was. He would tell her she deserved much more than what he could give her. She wasn't the type to indulge in a fling. Given what she'd revealed about her past and her childhood, it just wasn't in her nature. It would be unfair and cruel for him to pretend otherwise.

CHAPTER TEN

HOW FORMAL COULD a charity auction be? Jess decided the dress she'd worn last night would work for tonight's festivities, too. She'd freshen it up by hanging it in the bathroom as she took a steamy shower. It wasn't like she'd done much in it last night, just sat at a table then walked up on a stage where a little metal statue of a camera lens was handed to her. Plus, she happened to have packed a delicate, gold lace scarf that would serve to highlight the subtle golden detail in the fabric. Couple that with the huge gold hoops she hadn't worn last night, it was almost a completely new outfit.

Besides, the other option was the only other thing she'd packed—her little black dress, pretty boring now that she considered it in hindsight.

None of this had anything to do with the way Jordan had reacted to seeing her in the blue number last night.

Jess knew the exact moment Jordan had entered the main lounge area of his suite and was ready to go. Not that she could explain how she could sense such a thing. Somehow, she just did. The more time they spent together, the more in tune with him she seemed to be.

She was dressed and ready within an hour again, just as she was last night.

Jordan was waiting for her when she emerged. The tux he had on tonight was darker than yesterday's and appeared almost navy blue where the light hit it a certain way. It brought out the dark specks of his eyes in a subtle yet noticeable way. He held his arm out to her.

"Again. You look phenomenal, Ms. Raffi. I like the hair down that way. And that dress may as well have been made specifically for you. But did you perhaps forget to pack a second dress?"

Jess blinked at him. Did he like the dress or not? "I packed two dresses. I just happen to really like this one."

Jordan studied her up and down. She knew she wasn't imagining the appreciation she saw in his eyes. "There's no denying it flatters you. But if you're unhappy with the second choice, I did mention there's a boutique downstairs, fully at your disposal. It's your decision, of course."

Damned right it was. So why were they even having this conversation?

"I don't need to visit your boutique, Jordan." She lifted her chin. "I'm ready to go."

He hesitated for the briefest moment, then simply offered her his elbow without another word.

A nagging sense of unease washed over her as they made their way downstairs. Jordan was smiling at her politely; nothing in his demeanor struck her as odd or unwarranted. But there was definitely something off in the air between them. It had appeared as soon as he'd mentioned the boutique again in his apartment. Well, it was much too late to second-guess any of it now. Within moments she was stepping out of the limo once more as she had last night.

Jess realized her mistake immediately. This event was different than the awards ceremony. Much different. Clearly, this was a much bigger deal. An actual red carpet led up to the wide glass door. Unlike the few photographers that had awaited them yesterday evening, an actual gaggle of paparazzi greeted them. The flash almost blinded her and she had to grab at Jordan's forearm to keep from stumbling. By the time they made it inside and to their table, Jess was more than ready to sit down.

"I'll take that drink a bit earlier tonight," she informed Jordan. He didn't have to call the server over this time; a young lady with a tray appeared almost immediately and handed them each a flute of bubbly champagne.

The auction started about half an hour later. Jordan bid an exorbitant amount on some type of sailing package she didn't know enough about boats to understand. He ended up winning it.

The auctioneer moved on to the next item just as a rather plump, short man in a tan suit and leather hat approached their table.

"Jordan, my dear boy." He spoke with a tangy Southern drawl. Texan, to be more specific. "I was hoping I would see you here. It's been a while." The man turned his attention to Jess even as he shook Jordan's hand.

"Nice to see you, too, Teddy." Jordan stood to greet him and Jess followed suit to be polite.

"And who is this lovely lady you have with you?" Teddy asked before Jordan even had a chance to start an introduction. Jess noticed how slurry he was pronouncing his words. His Texas accent didn't quite explain why his *L*s sounded more like *W*s. Teddy had clearly started imbibing much earlier in the evening. Though he seemed pleasant enough.

"Meet Ms. Jessalyn Raffi."

"Nice to meet you, Ms. Raffi," Teddy told her.

"Please call me Jess."

"All right, then," Teddy drawled. "Which agency you with, little lady?"

"Agency?"

He winked at her. "You don't want to tell me who represents you, then?"

Jess blinked at him in confusion.

"Jess isn't a model," Jordan explained. Well, that certainly told her a lot about Jordan's dating history, didn't it?

Teddy's eyebrows shifted upward. "She isn't?"

"She's a dear friend," Jordan responded.

"Uh-huh. Sure." Teddy studied her up and down before continuing. "In any case. Jess. I'm glad you're here. With Jordan."

She wasn't sure what to say to that and could

have sworn she heard Jordan groan then swear under his breath.

Teddy turned back to him and dropped a hand on Jordan's shoulder. "That other lady you were with wasn't being very understanding about your new circumstances now, was she?"

Jordan gave him a tight smile before responding. "Old history." His response was an obvious cue to let the subject drop.

Teddy didn't get the hint. "In fact, I think she was just being down right bi—"

"How about a cup of coffee, Teddy?" Jordan interrupted before he could finish.

Teddy threw his head back and laughed out loud. "Way too late for coffee, son. But come on by my table later. I have some projects we should discuss."

With that, Teddy sauntered away.

"Let's forget that even happened and enjoy the rest of the night, shall we?" Jordan suggested as they sat back down.

Right. As if she could do that. As if she could stop wondering about who this woman Teddy spoke of could be. And what had she been unreasonable about?

She couldn't even presume to make an educated guess. It's not like Jordan had shared enough about himself to even make speculation possible. Jess thought back to the picture she'd found in his desk earlier today. He certainly kept things close to his chest. When she really thought about it, how well did she really know Jordan? He hadn't told her much about himself.

He hadn't confided in her at all beyond the barest of facts.

He didn't want the evening to end just yet.

Jordan unbuttoned his collar as they drove back to the penthouse and glanced over to Jess in the seat next to him. Sweet heavens, she was beautiful. He couldn't deny he enjoyed spending time with her. Aside from the uncomfortable interlude with Teddy, he'd had a really fun evening. When was the last time he'd thought that about a charity auction? He couldn't think of a single one.

He wasn't ready to bid her good-night.

He helped her out of the car once they arrived. "What would you say to getting some air?"

She took in the scene around them. "That

sounds lovely. Though it's a little late for a walk, isn't it?"

He winked at her. "It's never too late to stroll around New York. Surely, you've heard it's the city that never sleeps."

She laughed. "Of course."

"But that's not what I had in mind. Follow me."

He led her to the front doors of his building and through the lobby, past the main elevators.

"Where are we going?" Jess asked, glancing back at the elevator panel behind them.

"Trust me."

He took her to the back of the building, past the service entrance and loading dock. The elevator shaft back here was much narrower. Using his key card, he summoned the car to the first floor.

"Curious about where I'm taking you?" he asked after they'd passed several floors.

"I'm guessing it's an alternate route to your penthouse? I can't imagine why, though."

"Hmmm. Good guess. But it's wrong."

He showed her a few moments later when they got off on the top floor then traveled up a flight of stairs to the metal door that led outside, a door that only a handful of people had access to and the means to unlock.

"Oh, my God," Jess shrieked as they stepped out onto the roof of the tall high-rise. "This is amazing." The high wind served to muffle her words somewhat but her meaning was clear.

Jordan took her by the hand and led her to a small enclosed area that housed some of the backup generators. The walls were just tall enough to block out some of the wind.

She turned to stare out into the horizon, her breath deep and heavy with excitement. Jordan didn't take time to think about what he was doing. He put his hands on her hips and pulled her to lean back against him, her back up against his chest. The scent of her teased his senses. A subtle floral scent with a hint of lavender.

They stood that way for several moments, just silently admiring the view.

"What do you think?" he finally asked her.

"I'm in awe."

Her reaction sent a ripple of pleasure through him. He liked that she was enjoying herself so much. He'd never brought a woman up here before. It hadn't even occurred to him to do so. But he'd decided he would bring Jess when he'd seen her watching the city out of the limo windows.

Several more moments went by in silence. Finally, Jess spoke again on a soft sigh. "I've been trying so hard not to ask."

He could guess what she meant. She was thinking of Teddy and the references the man had made. He rested his chin on her shoulder. "The answer isn't terribly complicated. I was in the middle of a relationship when my father became ill. Not a terribly serious one, but a relationship nonetheless."

"What happened?"

"I ended up as sole guardian of a six-year-old girl. The woman I was with wasn't terribly comfortable with the new status quo. She wasn't exactly secretive about it."

She shifted ever so slightly to look at him over her shoulder. Their faces were a hairsbreadth apart. "What did she want you to do?"

"Long story short, she gave me an ultimatum."

"I see."

"You must also see the choice I made. Not that there was any real choice. I wasn't going to leave Sonya in the care of strangers or a twenty-four-hour nanny service. Although…" He let the sentence trail off. What was the point in getting into the rest? No good could come of it other than him venting.

"Although what?" she prompted.

"Nothing. It's not important."

"Jordan, please tell me what happened. Everything. I need to know all about Sonya if I'm going to be working with her one on one."

She had a point there.

And it was so easy to talk to her, to know that she was listening and honestly cared. He'd had no one to confide in or vent to when Sonya had first arrived in his home. He'd felt utterly alone—his father and mother both gone, his bachelor friends with no idea how to relate, and the woman he'd been with less than interested. Now here was Jess asking him to unburden some of himself.

"I'm not sure I'd know where to start," he admitted.

"There's an old saying—the best place to start is at the beginning," she replied. "You mentioned you wanted Sonya to grow up in a smaller, less hectic setting. Because of her accident."

A brick suddenly lodged itself in Jordan's throat. He had to push past it in order to continue. He wanted to tell Jess all of it, needed to confide in her like no one else before.

"We were walking down Madison Avenue," he began. "I wasn't even holding her hand." He squeezed his eyes shut as the memory of that afternoon came surging back. He'd been so distracted. So focused on his own concerns. So damn self-centered.

"You have to understand. I knew next to nothing about taking care of a child. And yes, a big part of me was more than a little resentful at being handed such a daunting responsibility."

"Didn't you have a nanny service?"

"It was all so new. We hadn't found Elise yet. I was in the process of interviewing and determining shifts."

"What happened?"

"We'd just purchased a helium balloon for Sonya from some street vendor when my phone rang. I wouldn't even be able to tell you now who I was speaking with. It was obviously not terribly important."

"Oh, Jordan."

"I didn't even realize she'd started running toward the street. The balloon had slipped out of her hand and she'd gone chasing after it." A deep shudder ran through his center as he spoke. "We were told things could have been so much worse. That if the cabbie hadn't reacted as quickly as he did… The doctors actually said Sonya was lucky. She was a little banged up. But her X-rays showed nothing seriously damaged or broken."

She didn't interrupt. Just let him continue. "But then she started having issues hearing different sounds. Each time she watched TV, she'd insist the volume be turned up louder and louder. It was gradual at first. Then got more pronounced. After a while it started affecting her speech, as well."

He finally looked up, expecting to see derision and scorn written all over her face. But even in the darkness, all he saw was sadness and empathy. A slight sheen of moisture glistened in her eyes.

She asked the most obvious question. "Did the accident cause her hearing loss?"

Jordan thought hard about how to answer that

question. He knew what the doctors had told him. But he couldn't bring himself to believe it. "I honestly don't know, Jess. All I do know is that I don't think I'll ever be able to forgive myself. For letting that child down so badly when she needed me the most."

Jess moved toward him, then wrapped her arms around him and simply held him tight.

Jordan couldn't guess how long they stood there. Time seemed to stand still. The noise of the wind and the city below grew muffled and muted. He didn't want any of it to end, just wanted to seek solace in the comfort of her embrace.

Finally, he felt her breathe out a deep sigh before she spoke his name. "Jordan?"

"Yes?"

"You told me that you'd leave it to me. Whether we would kiss or when."

His heart started to pound in his chest at where her words might be leading. "Yes?"

"And I've decided."

"You have?"

She nodded slowly. "Yes. I'd like for you to kiss me now. I'd like that very much."

Jordan didn't need to be asked twice. Taking

her about the waist, he pulled her up against his length. "A deal is a deal."

Then he crushed his lips to hers. And he was lost. Lost in the feel of her. Lost in the taste of her. Her soft moan of pleasure nearly had him undone. But he couldn't break away, was convinced his soul would shatter if he did.

He hadn't expected this, hadn't meant for it to happen. Though he was helpless against it now. In this moment she was air and light. And right now she was his. Her hands traveled up to his shoulders and held on tight. In response, Jordan deepened the kiss even farther. He couldn't get enough of her and perhaps he never would.

Jess was the one to finally pull away and he had to clench his hands by his sides to keep from reaching for her and pulling her back. Every last bit of this had to be her decision. Or he'd never forgive himself.

So her words when she spoke sent a spear of thrill right through his very core.

"Jordan, I'd very much like you to take me downstairs to your apartment now."

Jess could hardly think. The next few moments were a desire-filled haze as Jordan led her back to his penthouse. Then he started kissing her again as soon as the door shut behind them.

A wealth of emotion bubbled in her center at what he'd just confided. Emotion so overwhelming that she thought she might burst with it. But she held herself steady for Jordan's sake. He needed her strength right now. And her understanding. She wasn't going to bother with platitudes about how he shouldn't blame himself. Nor would she bother to point out that the accident had occurred when he was still reeling from the loss of his father and that he could be forgiven for being distracted at such a time.

Didn't he see just how overwhelmingly his life had been turned upside down through no fault of his own?

There was no use in trying to point it out to him. Not now. He wasn't ready or willing to hear any of it, she knew. Jordan would have to work his way to those conclusions on his own and in his own time. She would help in any way she could as he struggled with the reality of what he'd just confided. No matter how long it took.

But there was tonight. She didn't have much to give, but tonight she could offer him some comfort. Tonight she could be the woman Jordan wanted, not the woman that so many of those in her life had found so lacking. Tonight she was enough. For one night she wouldn't be the little girl who was abandoned by a mother who didn't want to change her lifestyle for her daughter. Nor would she be the teenager who'd been sent away by a father who'd never wanted her. And she would not be the college grad who'd had to return a ring to her fiancé because he'd suddenly found her to be far less than what he wanted in life. Or a visiting tourist's summer fling who didn't even warrant a simple goodbye.

Tonight would be different. Tonight would be about only the two of them.

"Jess." He whispered her name against her lips, his voice full of longing. Longing for her. "Tell me this is what you want."

She gripped his shoulders, tried to get her brain to function well enough to form a coherent answer. Somehow, she managed. "Yes. More than anything. More than I can say."

The last few words barely left her mouth and she felt herself being lifted off the ground. Jordan carried her through the hallway and to his bedroom. He set her down gently near his bed, all the while consuming her in another soul-shattering kiss.

She'd wanted this from the moment she'd first laid eyes on him. She'd wanted his arms around her, his lips tight against hers. But the reality was so much more than she'd imagined. The taste of him flooded her senses. And all she could think was that it wasn't enough.

She could only cry out his name. He responded by moving impatient hands along the sides of her body, up higher to her shoulders.

For some reason he tore his lips from hers and she thought the loss would break her.

"Jess? Are you sure, sweetheart?" he asked again, his voice full of longing. He was being touchingly careful with her, making sure to ask yet again if this was what she wanted.

Her answer was to slowly slide the straps of her dress off her shoulders and let it slip off her onto the ground.

Jordan sucked in his breath. Wrapping her arms around his neck, she pulled him up against her. Her need for him had reached a near maddening apex. "Now, Jordan. Please."

He obliged at once.

Jess turned herself over to him completely, let the pleasure of his touch and kiss burn through her from inside and out. The world ceased to turn. Only the two of them existed. All that mattered was the here and now.

CHAPTER ELEVEN

WHEN JESS WALKED into the kitchen the next morning, the world was different. Everything had changed. She'd spent the night in Jordan Paydan's bed. No matter what happened from here on out, the reality of that was the simple truth. More important, she was beginning to see through the surface to the man he truly was.

Jordan stood in front of the kitchen counter by the coffeepot as if willing it to brew faster.

He finally noticed her presence behind him. "Good morning."

"Morning," she responded with a shy smile. She didn't have much experience with morning-afters. In fact, aside from Gary and that one summer, she didn't have much experience in general.

"Coffee should be ready in a few minutes," he informed her then turned back to the pot.

Jess grappled for something appropriate to

say. It wasn't easy. And she blundered it royally. "I wanted to thank you for last night," she began, before it occurred to her how the statement might be misconstrued. She quickly explained. "I mean for taking me to the roof, that is. Not for—you know."

Oh, dear. That didn't sound much better. She was really messing this up.

Jordan simply chuckled but his laugh held no real amusement. The lines of his face were set tight, his jaw clenched.

Taking a deep breath, she tried again. "I won't soon forget how utterly magical the city looks from up that high. I wanted you to know that."

He came over to her and rubbed a finger softly down her cheek. She had to suppress a shudder at his touch. Memories of the previous night flooded her mind before she could do anything to stop it.

"You're welcome, Jess. Maybe I can take you up there again sometime."

Wow. So that was how they were going to play this next round.

He wasn't even sure if he would ever bring her back here, to his original home. Would she ever get another opportunity to travel back to

New York with him? What did it mean for her heart that she wasn't sure of the answer? So many questions that had to be answered in this new reality. Well, she was a big girl. One who would have to accept fully the consequences of the decisions she'd made last night.

"Do you have access to the roof because you own the penthouse?" she asked by way of conversation.

Jordan cleared his throat. "Not quite."

Jess raised her eyebrows in question.

Jordan shrugged in a distracted, casual gesture that belied his next words. "I have access because I own the whole building. Along with several other buildings like it throughout Manhattan and the Upper East Side."

Jess felt her jaw drop. "You own the entire building? And other similar ones?"

"That's right. My family's main source of income is prime New York real estate." His gaze searched her face. "I guess that never came up."

No. It certainly had not. She'd known Jordan was well-off. That fact was obvious to the naked eye. But apparently, he was more than just wealthy. Turned out he was a billionaire.

"No. It certainly didn't come up." She would have remembered.

He studied her reaction before turning away to the coffeepot. It was hard not to notice that he didn't offer her a cup this time, unlike yesterday.

"Help yourself to some coffee," he told her instead.

Jess wanted to hit the reset button on this whole morning. Instead of waking to find herself alone, she wanted to find a way to ensure he was there when she opened her eyes. Maybe Jess might have then found a way to entice him into staying under the covers a little longer.

Maybe they could have somehow avoided this whole awkward and strange conversation about his family finances.

She was about to admit to all that when his next words stopped her.

"I have the car coming for you in about half an hour," he told her. "I figured you're probably ready to be back home."

She was? And when exactly had he decided that for her? Without so much as speaking to her about it.

"What about you?" she asked.

"I've decided to stay back another day. Sonya's well taken care of with Elise. They usually just spend Sundays by the pool or reading. And there are some work issues that could use more of my attention before I leave the city."

Jordan wasn't even going to ride back to Massachusetts with her. For all practical purposes, he was sending her away. Like an errant child.

Jess tried to clamp down on the wealth of disappointment and sheer hurt that flooded her chest.

He nodded solemnly, then rubbed a hand down his face. "Speaking of Sonya, I hope the events of the past couple of days won't make you change your mind. About working with her."

Had he really just asked her that? Jess had to find her voice before she could answer. "Of course not."

Just the fact that he was asking such a thing made her realize just how little he really knew her, despite all they'd shared over the past two days. And all they'd shared last night. Despite their heartfelt conversation on the roof and the intimacy it had all led to. Perhaps it was even an indication of how little he thought of her. To think just a moment ago she'd believed she was actually beginning to know and understand him.

"Good. I'm glad to hear it."

"Did you really think I might do that to her?"

He lifted his shoulders in a slight shrug. "I didn't want to assume."

"I wouldn't let Sonya down that way."

She decided to focus on the practical rather than the heaviness that had suddenly gripped her chest in the area of her heart. "I can get a car service, Jordan. You don't have to have your personal driver waste a trip just for me."

His gaze hardened on her face. "I insist."

Of all the things she wanted to argue with him about at the moment, her ride back ranked pretty low in importance.

"I guess I'll go pack, then."

She'd never been one to overstay her welcome.

Jordan watched Jess walk out of the kitchen and toward her suite of rooms and resisted the urge to call her back. As soon as she shut the door behind her, he slammed his ceramic coffee mug hard enough against the Italian marble counter that a hairline crack appeared down its side.

What was there to say if he did call her back? He'd awoken this morning to a text message asking when he'd need the car to bring them back to Massachusetts. The message had served to remind him that reality was about to descend upon the sweet little fantasy he'd indulged in for the past forty-eight hours.

His life no longer consisted of regular charity auction balls or afternoons in Times Square. He had more responsibility on his shoulders now. He'd forgotten that last night. He could only hope to atone for it somehow. He could only hope to make Jess understand.

He'd never been one for one-night stands. And Jess was the last person in the world who deserved that from him. But there was no way for them to continue any type of relationship when they returned to their everyday lives. He'd lost sight of that reality last night.

That made him a unique sort of bastard.

He should have known better. He should have reminded himself that he was spread perilously thin already. There was no excuse for his lack of control—both physically and when he'd unburdened himself to her. Nothing but selfishness had motivated him. He couldn't deny that if he tried. Regardless of how he was beginning to feel about Jess, he had nothing left to give.

That was the only reason he was sending her away. A damning little voice inside his head wanted to argue that point. The same voice that had pestered him all night as he'd lain awake, thinking of the woman in his arms and how suddenly and unexpectedly she'd become so important to him. The same voice that was telling him he was merely being a coward.

Maybe the voice was right. None of it mattered. He'd never get over it or forgive himself if anything else happened to damage Sonya any further.

He could only hope he hadn't just done something to damage Jess.

Back to reality. Manhattan seems a lifetime ago rather than the week that had passed. Jess rummaged through the paperwork on her metal teacher's desk and tried to focus on the budgetary numbers Clara wanted her to take some time this weekend to look over. But focus eluded her. It was hard not to think for the hundredth time this morning about the two days she'd spent in the city with Jordan. A true fantasy. None of it had been real. Not for Jordan anyway, as evidenced by the fact that he hadn't so much as called or tried to contact her. She'd been to the mansion to visit Sonya twice already as they'd agreed. Jordan had been nowhere to be found. Maybe he was avoiding her. Maybe he'd even stayed in New York all this time, leaving Sonya in Elise's good hands.

That possibility stung at her eyes and she had to sniffle back unwanted tears.

So she thought she'd imagined it when his voice sounded from the doorway. There was no reason for Jordan to be here on a Saturday.

"Can I come in?"

She blinked up at him in surprise. Of all the ways she'd expected to run into him again, having him stop by her classroom on a rare Saturday morning that she was there hadn't been one of the possibilities that occurred to her.

Jess waved him in with her hand. To her further surprise, he shut the door behind him.

"Jordan?"

"Hey, do you have a minute? What are you doing here on a Saturday morning anyway?"

She gestured to the binders of figures in front of her. “Clara asked me to look at some of the center’s numbers. We have to make some budget cuts, unfortunately.”

He stepped farther into the room. “I’m sorry to hear that. That’s right, you mentioned you had a finance degree.”

She grunted a small laugh. “I do, indeed.” A degree she had pursued simply to prove she was different than her mother. Only to find that her artistic side was just as strong and needed to be nurtured. And that she didn’t have to become like her mother to do so.

“Yet, here you are. Teaching art to first-graders and working on a community center’s budget.”

“Yes, well. Life is full of surprises, as they say. But I’m sure you’re not here to discuss my college major or my uncertainty regarding career choices,” she said, pushing the binder away. “How did you find me anyway?”

“You weren’t answering your phone. So I called Clara and asked if she knew where you were.”

“You—you were asking about me?”

He didn’t answer her question. Rather, he

asked one of his own. One that didn't really make any sense. "Have you been online yet this morning?"

She shook her head. "No, I came straight here after grabbing a cup of coffee at Marilou's. Why?"

Jordan blew out a deep breath, looked away out the window. "That's why I'm here."

Okay. "You're here because of something you saw online?"

"That's right."

Her confusion started to turn into mild annoyance. For him to seek her out and come to find her in the classroom on a Saturday morning after end of session, without so much as acknowledging her for days, made absolutely no sense. "Jordan, what's this all about?"

He walked over to her side of the desk to stand next to her, then pulled her laptop closer and tapped a few keys. Jess wanted to hold her breath to keep from breathing in the distinctive scent of aftershave that had haunted her since that night in New York. Turned out she didn't need to, for what he showed her onscreen knocked the breath out of her.

She was trending!

Or rather, she'd inspired the trending term: *Same dress.*

"Oh, my."

Jess leaned in to look more carefully and scrolled through the various posts. Photos of her and Jordan were plastered all over the screen along with some very unflattering captions about her.

Out with one of New York State's most eligible bachelors... Why the same dress both nights?

One of the richest men in this hemisphere... can his date afford...?

Mystery lady with Jordan Paydan can't be bothered with another outfit...

Jess felt her pulse pounding through her veins. Great. Just great. The whole world was talking about her. Correction, they were making fun of her. Wait till the parents of her pupils got a load of all this. And her mother!

He should just go ahead and say it. That he'd tried to tell her. He'd tried to convince her to get a more suitable dress at the boutique in his building. And he literally owned the building. But her pride had made her stubborn that night and she'd said no.

To think she'd actually entertained the notion that she could fit into the life of someone like Jordan Paydan. How could she have forgotten who she was? How could she have lost sight of the fact that she didn't belong in his world? The women who did belong there never wore the same outfit twice, let alone to two consecutive events. She'd been fooling herself to think she could be enough for someone like him. As if she needed any more proof given the way he'd been avoiding her since they'd been intimate.

"Jess, I'm really sorry." Jordan spoke through her thoughts. "I should have seen this coming. I tend to get a bit of attention every time I'm seen with someone new."

She bit back a harsh retort at that comment. So now she was simply *someone new* as far as he was concerned. Someone for the New York tabloids to make fun of at her expense in their quest to achieve a few clicks.

Just further salt in the wound.

"Why are you here, Jordan?" she asked again, not even bothering to hide her irritation. "Did you want to tell me that you told me so? That I should have listened to your advice and let you donate me a dress?"

He blinked at her in confusion. "What? Of course not. And donate is certainly the wrong word."

"Is it?"

"Yes!" he said in a loud voice that echoed off the ceiling. He pointed to the screen. "And I'm only here because I wanted to show you this, to give you a heads-up that it's happening."

"You could have called me to warn me. Instead, you asked Clara where I was and made it a point to come find me. So you still haven't answered my question."

He rammed a frustrated hand through the hair at his crown. "Maybe I didn't want you to have to face it alone when you first saw it? Is that such a mystery?"

She shrugged. "Maybe. One thing for certain—*you* definitely are a mystery."

His eyes narrowed on her. "What's that supposed to mean?"

"It means I can't figure you out."

"What puzzle about me are you trying to unravel, Jess?"

Her jaw dropped at the question "Are you serious? You really need to ask me that? Since you've arrived in this town, you've kept yourself completely closed off. But when we spend any time together, you're warm and giving, the most dynamic man I've ever been with. Then you seem to completely shut down again. I don't see you for days." She had to swallow past the lump that had suddenly formed in her throat. "I guess I was just hoping..."

"What?"

"I was hoping that pattern would break after the night we spent together in your penthouse."

A wealth of emotion clouded his eyes. But perhaps she had imagined it, for the very next moment they hardened with a glint of steel.

"You're right."

"I am?"

He nodded. "In that we needed to talk about what happened that night."

Part of Jess wanted to kick herself for bringing on this conversation. There was no doubt she was going to hate what she was about to hear. Well, she'd never been one to shirk unpleasantness if it was necessary.

"So let's talk, then," she prompted, bracing herself for what was to come.

He drew in a deep breath, didn't quite meet her eyes. Oh, yeah. This was going to be bad.

"I've never been one for serious relationships, Jess. And I certainly am in no place right now in my life to start."

"I see."

"Though I'm not going to apologize for what happened between us. I don't regret it."

Her mouth went dry. "You'd be insulting me if you did."

"But I should have been more up-front about what to expect. I have no excuse. Except that I thought you knew. That you were aware enough about me."

"What makes you think I didn't know?"

That her questions surprised him was clear in his expression.

"Huh? But that next morning..."

"That was just me being honest with you, Jordan. I tend to be pretty open with my feelings. I'm sorry if that scared you."

"I didn't say I was scared."

And there it was, the denial. He was probably even denying to himself. She wouldn't point it out to him. There was really no reason to. "Fine. We won't call it scared. We'll call it not ready."

"We'd be right to call it that."

“So you’re essentially saying it’s the wrong place and the wrong time. For us.”

“Yes. That’s exactly what I’m saying.”

She tapped her chin with her finger. “And just so I’m clear. You’re also saying that what happened between us in Manhattan was a fling. Meaningless.”

His jaw tightened. “Don’t put words in my mouth, Jess. That’s not what I said.”

“Which is it, then, Jordan? It sounds like you haven’t quite made up your mind.”

He spread his arms out wide in a clear motion of exasperation. “What do you want me to say? I can’t figure out what you want to hear. I only came down to make sure you were okay if you’d seen the tabloids about your dress.”

“This seems to be a waste of both our time.” She picked up her pen again. “If you’ll excuse me, I have work to do. Thank you for letting me know about the unflattering hashtag.”

But he made no move to go. Just stood there, staring at her with his mouth agape. “That’s it? That’s all you’re going to say?”

“What more is there to say? And why should I bother when you’re not going to really answer me?”

"What questions would those be? I seem to have missed them somehow."

She gave a slow shake of her head. "You didn't miss them. You chose to ignore them. Questions like why you care enough to worry about my reaction to unflattering posts about me but not enough to call me during the week after we spend forty-eight magical hours together. Or why you would go out of your way to make sure I had a weekend with you that I would never forget—between taking me to a Broadway show and later treating me to a rooftop view of the Manhattan night—only to turn around and pretend none of it meant anything to you."

She wasn't expecting the depth of disappointment that suddenly flooded his eyes. Damn it. What did any of it mean? Rubbing a hand down her face, she blew out a harsh breath. She was just so completely off her guard when it came to this man.

"Did it occur to you that I might not have the answers, Jess?"

"Oh, Jordan." But he'd already turned to leave. He didn't give her another look back as he shut the door softly behind him.

CHAPTER TWELVE

THAT HAD GONE WELL, Jordan thought with sarcasm as he pushed open the door that led out to the parking lot. What had he expected, though? That Jess would jump up into his arms and thank him for alerting her to the reports? Hell, he was the reason she was all over social media to begin with. He hadn't even apologized for it. And now he may not get a chance. Something made him halt before walking out. He sensed her presence behind him down the hallway.

"Jordan, wait."

He had to acknowledge the hefty feeling of relief that surged through him. It hadn't felt right to leave things as they were between them.

"What do you want me to do?" she asked, walking slowly toward him until they were only a few feet apart.

What exactly was she asking him? There were myriad ways he could answer that question; all sorts of things he could think of that he wanted her to do. Like wrap her arms around him. Let him take her mouth in a possessive kiss the way he'd been dreaming about since they'd returned to the island. Oh, yeah, all sorts of ways he could respond about exactly the things he wanted her to do.

"About the SM posts," she clarified. "I realize I must have embarrassed you." She swallowed down hard. "I'm sorry about that."

What? Why in the world was she the one apologizing to him? Nothing made sense anymore.

"What are you talking about, Jess?" She squinted at him as if what she was referring to should be obvious. "What on earth do you have to apologize for?"

"The way your name is splattered all over the web. Because I don't know how to dress for gala parties in Manhattan."

He could only stare at her, his mouth agape. "You think this is somehow your fault? The fact that you're being ridiculed and taunted by the New York tabloids?"

"Isn't it? After all, you tried to get me to visit the boutique. And you certainly weren't the one who wore the same dress two nights in a row," she quipped with a hint of a smile. A smile so enticing, he lost his train of thought as images of taking her lips with his own flooded his brain and heated him through to his core. Even dressed as she was, in loose, baggy capri sweatpants and a thinning baseball jersey, Jess was so damn pretty. Her thick, luscious hair was piled high on top of her head. Just enough strands had escaped their hold that they framed her lovely face. She wore no makeup and didn't appear to have showered just yet. That thought led to another unwelcome one as he imagined her stepping naked into a bath. He was there with her, helping her lather up and rubbing the soap all over her body.

Stop it!

When he finally spoke, he said the only words that came to his mind. "You fool. You silly, beautiful, guileless fool."

Her eyes grew wide. But then she looked up at the ceiling with a resounding laugh. "I guess you and I tend to interpret things differently."

"I guess so."

"I'm not sure what to do about that."

Neither did he. But he knew what might be

a good way for them to start. "Can you break away for a few minutes, Jess? Just to talk?"

She sucked in her bottom lip, giving it serious thought. To the point where Jordan was afraid she was about to turn him down.

But ultimately, she nodded. "There's a raggedy, uncomfortable wooden bench by a small stream behind the building. I sit out there to sketch sometimes."

Another flood of relief surged through him that she hadn't turned down his offer. "That sounds lovely. It's a beautiful day out."

"All right. I'll even treat you to bad vending machine coffee and we can take it out there."

He couldn't help himself; he stepped closer to her. They stood within inches of each other. He gently rubbed a finger down her cheek. She trembled at the contact, making him wish he could touch her further. Really touch her.

He hadn't wanted to admit to himself just how much he'd missed her these past few days. "That's the best offer I've had in a while," he said on a hoarse whisper. Why had he even tried to stay away from her? Jordan followed Jess to a small break room with an automatic coffee server on the counter and a mostly empty vending machine against the wall. Jess turned the coffeepot on then stepped over to the snack vending machine and punched in a code. A package of sugary chocolate cupcakes fell to the bottom.

She grabbed it and held it out. "I'll share this with you."

"Another tempting offer. You spoil me."

Within moments they were outside sitting on her wooden sketching bench. The narrow stream meandered lazily by their feet. The seat was much too small and he was certain he'd stand up with more than a few splinters in his backside. The half a cupcake Jess offered him was stale and much too rich. And he had to resist the urge to spit out the watery, tasteless coffee. If one could even call the beverage that.

Jordan had sat in deluxe cafés by the Seine indulging in chef-prepared desserts and gourmet espresso ground from the finest java beans.

But at this moment there was nowhere else he'd rather be.

"This is quite a view," Jordan commented as they sat down. Jess had drawn this particular landscape countless times during her time working for the community center. The scenery changed with the seasons, providing her with a varying subject every time. She took in the lush greenery now, the bright sunshine, the pretty ferns that grew along the base of the stream. A red-chested robin watched them from a tree branch above.

"It is, isn't it? Though it doesn't quite compare to the lit-up Manhattan skyline from a high rooftop."

Jordan continued to study the picturesque scene in front of them. "It's equally as stunning. In a different way."

Jess breathed in deep. The air out here always seemed to exhilarate and refresh her. "The flora is different. But something about it reminds me of the Malaysian landscape."

"You've been to Malaysia?"

She sighed as the memories resurfaced. "Yes. Once. To visit my father."

Jordan turned to her in surprise. "I didn't think he was very present in your life."

Accurate. "He wasn't. But my mother had me stay in touch with him and send him letters as soon as I learned how to read and write. Present or not, she was adamant that I knew I had a father."

"I see."

"He was nice about writing back. More of a pen pal, really. So when I turned sixteen, I asked my mom to let me go visit him as a sweet sixteen present. She obliged." Jess humphed out a small laugh. "She probably figured it was an easy way to acknowledge such a major birthday without having to travel herself to come see me."

Jordan reached for her hand and took it in his own. Though it most definitely wasn't wise given the past week, Jess allowed his touch. Welcomed it, in fact.

"Sorry to hear that, Jess."

The empathy in his voice sent a curl of warmth through her chest. "I don't know what I was thinking asking to see him. He'd never really been more of a pen pal. My first clue should have been his less than enthusiastic reply when I wrote to tell him I'd be flying in."

"I take it the visit didn't go well."

Again, accurate. "You're right. It was a fiasco from day one. By the time I returned to the States a week later, I was more than ready to be back. And I have no doubt my father was ready to have me go."

"What happened?"

His fingers gave hers a tight, reassuring squeeze. And it felt good. Talking to him felt good. She'd wondered all week when she'd see him again next. The scenario of the two of them sitting on her wooden park bench hadn't exactly been one of her guesses.

"Nothing terribly surprising," she answered. "By then he'd moved on, gotten married. Had two daughters and one son all several years younger than I was. I felt like a complete fish out of water staying at his house with them."

"Oh, Jess. That was terribly unfair to you."

"Maybe. I think his family thought the opposite. That I was being unfair to them."

"What? That makes no sense."

Jess hadn't forgotten the pain of it. She'd been carrying it with her for over a decade, after all. The utter sense of rejection, of not being wanted. She'd felt that before during her childhood years. The various maternal relatives she'd been hoisted upon often made no secret that they'd only taken her in out of a sense of family responsibility.

But the sting of being rejected by your own parent, your flesh and blood, carried a stronger bite.

"They seemed to feel I was flaunting my very existence by being there. The wife was particularly resentful." She blew a strand of hair off her face. "I wish she'd just been up-front about her objection to my visit from the get-go."

"Sometimes wives in that part of the world don't have much of a say in decisions made by their husbands."

"I considered that. She just passive-aggressively shunned me when I was there."

"Did you have any fun while you were there?" Jordan asked with genuine concern in his voice.

"My half siblings were nice enough. Except for the youngest one—the little boy—did keep asking me why I was there. Purely innocently. But it was just one more way the whole trip was awkward and stressful from the beginning."

He rubbed the top of her hand with his thumb. "You didn't deserve that, Jess. Particularly not at the already tumultuous age of sixteen."

"Thank you for saying that." She took comfort in those words. "That's why Sonya's so lucky to have you, Jordan. I've been wanting to tell you that."

Jordan didn't respond. Just continued to stare ahead at the scenery. "I mean, you've given her a stable home, genuine affection and you're making sure she knows she's wanted. I know she must appreciate that."

She felt Jordan's whole body suddenly go rigid. When he did finally turn to her, the pain in his eyes nearly took her breath away.

If he were at all a decent man, Jordan would stop Jess right now in the process of praising him and correct all her false assumptions. How could she even think such things after what he'd revealed to her in New York?

Jess continued, "Really, Jordan. Sonya's very fortunate not to be strapped to a parent or relative who doesn't want her."

Like she had been.

"She has you to thank for that," Jess added.

"She's my only sibling. My only family," he answered simply.

"And you're doing right by her. Despite all that you yourself had to go through."

"Is that how you see things?"

"I see the reality. You had so much to deal with after losing your mother. Then your father more recently."

"He became a different man after she died. It was like losing him, too." Jordan released a deep sigh. He remembered how frightened he'd been as a young teenager suddenly without the mom who'd cared for and cherished him. And how distant his father became as a result of her being gone.

Jess leaned ever so slightly into him. He wanted to pull her onto his lap to seek comfort in her warm embrace. Perhaps they'd be comforting each other, in fact.

"I would dare to say that you never got a chance to grieve your father," Jess seemed to say out of the blue.

He quirked an eyebrow in her direction. "I guess I never really gave it much thought. There were too many arrangements to be made."

"And a little girl to be taken care of." She inhaled. "Think about it, Jordan. Your father was gone and all of a sudden you were sole guardian to his other child. Did you ever get a chance to actually mourn his loss?"

"I guess not. Especially after..." His unspoken words hung in the air between them.

"Sonya's accident, you mean," Jess supplied.

He didn't really want to get into this again. A part of him wished he'd never told Jess about the accident in the first place. She clearly wanted to rehash it some more. And he absolutely didn't. "I'd rather not get into this again, Jess. There's no useful purpose in discussing it over and over."

She shaded her eyes, remained silent for a moment. But not for long. "I can respect that. But I need to say one more thing—you can't blame yourself, Jordan. It isn't healthy for either of you. Not for the accident. And certainly not for Sonya's developing disability."

Of course she wasn't going to let the subject drop. Not easily anyway. Jordan simply sighed, waited for her to continue. He regretted that decision as soon as she did.

"You have to realize that the accident wasn't your fault. You had a lot on your mind. Any new parent can easily become distracted. And someone in your position has even more of an excuse—"

A sudden, unexpected fission of annoyance

had him stiffening, and he cut her off midsentence. "If I wanted to be analyzed, I would have sought the services of a professional." There was no use in rehashing all this, any of it. It was all past history, which made no difference in his reality today.

Jordan bit out a curse at her responding gasp. Like he thought earlier, if he could only be a more decent man.

"I'm sorry, that was uncalled for. It's just… I'm not really used to talking about all this."

"I kind of got that impression our last morning in Manhattan."

"I'm sorry," he apologized once more, not sure what else to do.

She sucked in her bottom lip. "Just so you know, believe it or not, I've never shared that Malaysia experience with anyone. Not even Kelly. And especially not my mother."

That revelation had him torn between being flattered and feeling unworthy. "I'm glad you did tell me."

They sat in silence for several minutes. Jordan wanted to brush off all the things she'd just said and the points she'd made about his father. The loss of his mother. It could be argued that he'd never actually gotten a chance to grieve for her, either. His father had just been so broken that Jordan felt the need to be the strong one, the stoic one.

And as responsible as he felt about the accident, every doctor they'd visited had emphasized that Sonya's hearing loss couldn't be attributed to it. But he couldn't bring himself to tell Jess she might be right on that score. Just as he couldn't bring himself to fully believe it.

Dear heavens. He hadn't thought about any of this with any great depth. Didn't want to do so now. How had they even started along this path?

Finally, Jess broke the silence. "You never answered me."

Jordan felt a tingle of trepidation in his chest. He wasn't sure how much more of a heart-to-heart he could take right now. "About what?"

"Whether you want me to address the online activity."

The sudden change in topic threw him off and it took some effort to try and redirect his focus.

"Should I post something?" she asked.

"That won't be necessary."

"Are you sure? It can't look good for you."

Leave it to her to be concerned about his reputation when hers was the one being publicly ridiculed. "It's all right, Jess. I have people working on it. You don't have to do anything personally."

"What kind of people?"

"Pros whose job it is to track and try and influence social media."

"Huh. What exactly are they doing?"

He gave her a small shrug. "A handful of responders to the tabloids were complimentary toward you. Some admired your resourcefulness. Others pointed out you were setting a good example about reusing."

Her eyebrows lifted. "They did?"

"My people are making sure those posts outtrend the less flattering ones."

"Huh."

"I just wanted you to be aware of it. So that you didn't find out the hard way after going online."

"I see." She stood and stretched out her legs. Jordan followed. "Well, I should get back to those binders. It's going to take me all afternoon to figure out where the budget should be cut."

"Can I help in any way?"

Jess shook her head. "Part of the problem is that Clara keeps everything on paper hard copies. Not that we could afford a computer system anyway."

They slowly made their way back through the tall grass. They'd just gone over a lot of territory. He needed some time to process. Besides, she had work to do cutting a budget.

An idea occurred to him just then. Maybe she wouldn't need to slash the center's budget, after all.

Jess shut the door of her classroom behind her and leaned back against it taking deep breaths. She had no idea how long she'd stood there. But it was going to be near impossible to try and focus on numbers and budgets after Jordan's visit. Her concentration would be shot as she replayed their conversation over and over in her mind.

Not to mention the way he'd touched her, first with a finger down her cheek and then as he'd held her hand tight on the bench. She'd been intimate with the man and—though that intimacy had touched something deep within her soul—his mere gentle caresses could be just as affecting.

Oh, dear. She had it bad. She was in really deep.

And she hadn't even seen it coming. No wonder she was so woefully unprepared. Because all she wanted to do right now was to crumple to the floor and cry.

She'd somehow fallen head over heels for Jordan Paydan. And he was nowhere near ready to let her in. Not judging by the conversation they'd just had. Her heart would probably never recover.

The whole situation was impossible. She had no doubt Jordan wanted her still—as much as he had that night in New York. That much was obvious in the way he'd looked at her just now before he left. And it was obvious in the way he'd kept touching her. Jess knew she just only had to say the word and they'd have a replay of the night they shared. Her whole life had been spent trying to achieve a sense of emotional grounding and stability. Her quest for such stability had driven her once to pursue the wrong career and into the arms of the wrong man when she'd agreed to wed Gary. No, at this point in her life, she couldn't bring herself to have a meaningless fling.

And Jordan had made it blatantly clear than he wanted nothing more.

CHAPTER THIRTEEN

JORDAN TRIED TO be gracious as Clara Thompson served him yet another cup of the dreadful coffee he'd had the other day while sitting outside with Jess. Did anyone actually really drink this slop?

"This is so unexpected, Mr. Paydan," Clara said as she took a seat across from him at her desk. She motioned for him to take the chair opposite. Her office was small yet neat. Potted plants sat perched on various surfaces in each corner.

"Please call me Jordan."

The older woman gave him a wide smile. "Very well. Thank you, Jordan. We won't have to cut any of our programs as a direct result of your generosity. Even our summer sessions can stay intact."

Jordan cleared his throat. He always felt a little self-conscious when people thanked him profusely for a charitable contribution. The money meant so little to him in the overall scope of things. But it meant so much to organizations like the one Clara was a director for. He didn't want to see the community center lose any of its offerings when the solution was so simple.

"Well, when I heard you were looking into budget cuts, I knew right away what the very next check I wrote would be."

"I'm ever so thrilled that you did. And what a generous check it is. The staff will be thrilled to hear the news."

Jordan shifted in his chair. This was the reason he'd wanted to hand the check to Clara personally. "About that…"

"Yes?"

"I'd prefer if this were to remain between the two of us."

She blinked at him in surprise. "You would?"

"Yes, please."

"Do you mind if I ask why?"

He didn't mind her asking per se. But he had no intention nor the desire to get into it.

Jordan didn't want to explain that he didn't want for Jess to hear about this donation and try to read anything into it. Or try to thank him in some meaningful and sincere way that left them both feeling awkward. No, it was much better that she not find out.

"Let's just say I'd like to keep it as anonymous as possible."

She glanced down at the paper check yet again. "I see. I guess I can come up with some kind of story to tell folks."

"I have faith you will."

"Well, again, thank you so much for your generosity. It will go a long way."

"You're welcome, Clara. I'm glad to help."

"I guess I only have one other question."

"Ask away."

"Is there anything in particular you'd like some of the funds allotted for?" she asked with clear hesitation. The poor woman must have come to the conclusion that the money came with some type of strings attached given that Jordan didn't even want to publicize it. What did she think he might ask for? Maybe she thought he had a desire to see some type of specialty class offered like pickling autumn vegetables or straw hat weaving.

Jordan had to laugh. "Maybe a minor suggestion."

"What's that?"

"Would you consider replacing the coffee machine?"

"Jordan? I thought that was you walking out of Clara's office. I didn't think Sonya had any swim lessons today."

Jordan released a resigned sigh and turned to find Jess standing just a few short feet behind him. He'd been caught. He should have headed straight home. Instead, he'd felt compelled to walk back out to Jess's little wooden bench by the stream. The scene was just as pretty as it had been the other day. Especially now that she'd joined him out here. But now he had to explain his presence here to Jess.

"She doesn't."

"Then what are you doing here?"

He gestured to their surroundings. "Would you believe I had an unexpected desire to come out here again and see this view?"

She tilted her head back and studied him. Skepticism shone in her eyes. "I would definitely have trouble believing that. As serene as this spot is. Plus, that doesn't explain why you were in Clara's office."

"Uh, I just needed to ask Clara about some of the class offerings available next session." His reply was technically the truth. Also, the class offerings and their detailed descriptions were easily found in the online brochure, which, of course, she knew. For a brief moment she looked as if she wanted to say something. Luckily, however, she let the matter drop.

"Next session's classes don't start until September. But be sure to sign Sonya up early. They fill up quickly, especially considering we'll have to make some cuts so there won't be as many classes to choose from."

"I don't think that will be an issue any longer," Jordan stated before he could think to stop himself.

Her brows lifted in surprise. "Oh?"

The thick clouds threatening to dampen the day shifted over the sun, casting a grayness to the area. Jess's tone was clipped, professional. She was simply one of the center's instructors speaking to a parent. A brick seemed to have settled in Jordan's stomach. He had to clench his fists by his sides to keep from reaching for her, from taking her in his arms and kissing away the tightness in her lips.

Just then the phone Jess held in her hands sounded an incoming alert. "It's a text from Clara. She says she has some good news to tell me about."

Jordan watched her expression as she put two and two together. She was too sharp not to figure it out.

"Jordan. Do you have something you'd like to tell me?"

He wasn't going to lie to her. Releasing a sigh, he admitted what he'd just done. "I wanted to help out the center with a donation. The cuts can be avoided."

A clear glint of disappointment and sadness settled over her features. He wanted so badly to wash that disappointment away. He wanted to ask her to sit with him again on the rickety bench just to watch the stream trickle by. He wanted her to let him hold her hand again. There appeared to be a standoffish quality about her this morning. A distance she was putting between them; one that hadn't been there the last time they'd spoken to each other. But this Jess before him now seemed so different from the woman who had shared her story about visiting the father who didn't want to see her.

This Jess didn't seem at all likely to open herself up that way. Certainly not to him. Not now.

"How nice of you," Jess began, speaking through tight, gritted teeth. "You saw an issue and you wrote a check. Thanks so much," she added, her voice thick with sarcasm. Then she turned on her heel and began to walk back toward the building.

Jordan stayed silent and simply watched her walk away. Suddenly, the scene before him didn't seem quite as picturesque as it had just a few short minutes ago.

Jordan stood up from the European-style oak desk in his study and walked over to stare out the window. The clouds from earlier this morning had grown thicker, and the afternoon had grown darker.

Which matched his mood perfectly.

"Aren't you taking this brooding billionaire thing a little too far?" a feminine voice asked from behind him. He hadn't bothered to shut his door. Not like he was focusing much on work emails anyway.

"Hello, Elise."

She stepped into the room with a wave. "Sonya wanted me to come and see if you had any time later to watch her. She wants to show you some of her swim strokes she learned in her swim class."

Jordan glanced at his watch. "I have a conference call from Japan scheduled in about fifteen minutes. Should take about an hour. I'll come out then."

"I'll let her know. Oh, and she also asked that we invite her friend to come watch her, too. She's become quite the little show-off when it comes to her swimming. Apparently, I'm no longer sufficient enough an audience."

Jordan returned her chuckle. "That's fine. Invite however many little friends she wishes."

"Okay. But she's not little. Sonya wants Jess to come see her."

His laughter quickly faded. *Damn.* "I don't think that's such a good idea. Maybe they can see each other some other time."

"Is there a reason? Sonya will wonder why. She's actually been asking about Jess, wondering when her next art session will be."

Jordan tried to clamp down on his frustration

and annoyance. It wouldn't be fair to direct it toward Elise simply because she happened to be the bearer of Sonya's message. Nor could he blame his little sister. It made sense that she was wondering about the friendly teacher who'd shown her such kindness and warmth.

He wasn't quite successful. "Can't you just tell her Jess is busy or didn't answer her phone or something?" he asked, his tone more abrupt and clipped than he would have liked.

Elise lifted an eyebrow at him. "I'm not going to lie to her, Jordan. I've never done so and don't intend to start now. If that's the route you want to take, you're going to have to do so yourself."

He rammed a hand through his hair in frustration. Was every female put on this earth simply to vex him? "Fine, feel free to invite Ms. Raffi over to watch Sonya."

The telltale eyebrow lifted even higher. "She's Ms. Raffi to you, huh?"

"Your point?"

Elise actually walked over and shut the door. That couldn't bode well. Whatever she wanted to say, she apparently didn't want Sonya hearing it.

"Let's see," she began. "Sonya told me in detail about the fun evening the three of you spent at some type of ice cream novelty spot in town. I know you took her with you to attend the charity auction. Oh, and there were also pictures of you and her splashed all over the internet, some of which seemed like you were having quite a great time together."

"You saw the pictures, too, huh?"

"I tend to notice when my employer is a trending hashtag."

"Again, I ask if you have a point."

She threw her hands up in the air. "My point is I'm wondering why, after all that, you're referring to Jess so formally as Ms. Raffi and why you seem utterly aghast at the prospect of her stopping by." She suddenly stopped. "Unless…oh, my!"

Jordan swore once more, not bothering to try and conceal it this time. How was this any of his employed nanny's business? Jordan came close to asking her just that, but refrained. After all, the woman had completely altered her life to move out of the city to come settle in this rural town with them. He owed it to her to at least let her speak.

Elise went on, "I know I've only just met her, but from what I've seen, Jess Raffi is a genuine, kind and compassionate woman. So whatever went wrong, I'm guessing the blame falls squarely on your shoulders."

That settled it. There was no way Elise was getting any kind of raise anytime soon.

Not that he needed to explain himself, but Jordan found himself answering to her. "I don't know what you mean. Nothing happened that could go wrong." He said the last two words in air quotes.

Elise crossed her arms in front of her chest. "Really? Correct me if I'm wrong, but I'm guessing Jess started to get close so you closed yourself off."

She was out of line. Elise had only recently entered their lives. She knew nothing about the anguish he'd felt watching his father suffer. She hadn't heard the man asking for his young wife—a wife who had no desire to comfort the husband she'd vowed to honor and cherish.

And Elise hadn't been privy to the conversation when the woman Jordan had been dating for the better part of the year declared the relationship over, only because he refused to turn his back on a child he'd been entrusted with.

If Jordan's reaction to witnessing such betrayals was to become *closed off*, then it was no one's concern but his own.

That was it. He may owe it to Elise to listen but far enough was far enough. "Invite her over or don't. Frankly, I don't have the time nor the patience to deal with it. Now, if you'll excuse me. I have to make that call."

Elise didn't say another word, just turned to the door and walked out, her disappointment in him unmistakable in the rigid set of her shoulders.

Jordan slammed the phone down as she exited. Another person he had let down.

What was yet one more?

His sister was doing her best imitation of a fish when he walked out onto the patio an hour later. But Jordan's focus landed solely on the woman standing by the pool, clapping and cheering Sonya on.

Part of him felt glad to see her here, happy that she'd accepted Sonya's invitation. Another part wanted to turn back into the house. But his sister was expecting him. So here he was.

Jess wore another colorful sundress again today, this one a pale green with a soft billowy skirt that displayed just enough of her legs to make his palms itch. Strappy leather sandals adorned her feet and showed off bright pink polished toes. Jordan thought hard to recall the last time he'd noticed the color of a woman's toes and couldn't think of one.

Jess's laughter came to a sudden halt when she noticed Jordan approaching. A brick of disappointment landed in his gut at her reaction upon seeing him.

He walked over to where she stood. Elise didn't appear to be out here. Jess gave him a small wave then turned her gaze back to the water and Sonya's backstroke.

"Your little sister is apparently part guppy," she remarked when Jordan reached her side.

"I'd say at least sixty to seventy percent."

It was a lame joke but Jess indulged him with a small laugh. "She couldn't wait to show you all she's learned," he told her. "She's very glad you came, I'm sure."

"I'm honored she wanted to show me."

Jordan rammed his hands into his pockets. “Frankly, I’m a little surprised you came.”

Sonya chose that moment to pop her head out of the water and nod her head in a small bow. Jess clapped again.

“To be perfectly honest, I didn’t think you’d be here. Figured you’d be working. Elise didn’t mention you would be. In fact, she sort of alluded that you wouldn’t.”

Ouch. “She did?”

Jess nodded, her gaze still on Sonya, who’d started a series of butterfly strokes down the length of the pool.

“She probably figured you would say no if you knew about my presence,” Jordan told her.

“Should I have? Said no?”

“No.”

“Are you sure about that?”

He reached for her shoulders then and turned her to face him. She’d just been honest with him so one good turn deserved another. “Yes. I’m sure. Because I’m happy you’re here, too.”

CHAPTER FOURTEEN

JESS FELT LIKE a schoolgirl who'd just been acknowledged by her older teenage crush. Then she wanted to kick herself for feeling that way, for the way she reacted to this man whenever he was near. Her pulse quickened; excitement hummed through her veins. She had to get a hold of it. She had to get a hold of herself.

"Clara was bristling with excitement about all the programs we weren't going to have to cut, after all." Jess wasn't even aware she was going to bring up the subject until the words had left her mouth.

"Jess, the donation is separate from what's between you and me."

Jess's heart fluttered in her chest. Her pulse quickened. She knew she should let that be the final say, had sworn to herself that she wouldn't subject her heart to the potential pain. But Jess had to ask her next question. "How exactly would you define that, Jordan? What's between you and me?"

He bit out a curse. "Damned if I've figured it out."

She was about to tell him that wasn't enough. That he had to at least try to formulate some answers. He owed her that much. But the screen door to the kitchen sounded open just then. Elise walked out to the patio carrying a tray of lemonade.

"Who wants some refreshments?" She set the tray down on an outdoor table next to them then motioned to her charge who had popped up out of the water for a breath.

"She's going to prune if she doesn't come out now."

It took several moments but Sonya finally heeded Elise's urges to climb out of the pool. Jess gave her another round of applause when she exited the water. Elise wrapped her up in a large, thick towel. "Let's go get you dry and dressed."

"I guess the show is over," Jordan stated when the other two had left.

Great. They had to endure another one of the

awkward silences that seemed to be so prevalent between them.

"I should be going. Tell Sonya I'm very proud of her. Truly."

"You haven't had your lemonade. Elise will be out of sorts. She makes it homemade."

It appeared this was going to be the afternoon Jess figured out how quickly she could drain about twelve ounces of sour citrus. She eyed the drink warily. Elise had served it in very tall glasses.

"Try some," Jordan urged.

Jess picked up one of the glasses and took a large sip. An explosion of sweet and tart filled her mouth. "Wow. This is really good."

He smiled in pleasure then reached for his own drink. "I told you. Have a seat."

Jess hesitated but eventually did as he said. What would it hurt to spend a few minutes with him as she enjoyed a refreshing lemonade that someone had worked so hard to prepare?

The question seemed to mock her when Jordan came to sit next to her on the wicker settee. He looked so handsome out in the bright sun. His collar was undone; the sleeves of his dress shirt had been rolled up above his elbows.

Curse the man for being the most appealing one she'd ever encountered. And the scent of him, now so familiar yet still oh-so-tempting.

His body next to hers sent a wave of warmth over her skin and she took another long, deep gulp of her drink to try and cool down. It didn't help in the least.

"I guess we should talk about a schedule for Sonya's art lessons."

Jordan cleared his throat. "About that. I wanted to run an idea by you."

"What sort of idea?"

"I was thinking about what you said about Sonya perhaps benefitting from an art therapist."

Something in his tone sent alarm bells ringing in her head. "I'm listening."

"I think it might be good for her to work with one at some point."

She took another swig of her drink. "I don't disagree. But what's that got to do with me?"

"I wanted to ask you if you'd be interested in pursuing it yourself. As a career. I've done some research. With your background as an instructor, it shouldn't take much time for you to become certified. Of course, I'd be taking care of the costs and fees associated with the training, as well as tuition for the required classes. As a potential future employer, that is."

Jess felt the anger slam into her chest like a spear. "Just to be clear—you're offering to pay to have me trained and licensed as an art therapist. So that I can come work for you in that capacity at some point."

He nodded once. "That's exactly right. I wouldn't expect Sonya to be your only client. We can negotiate—"

She didn't let him continue. Slamming the glass so hard down on the table that a resounding thud echoed through the air, she stood and whirled around to directly face him.

"Damn you, Jordan Paydan. Damn you for doing this. How do you still not get it?"

He blinked up at her from his seated position in horrified shock. The look did nothing to assuage her ire. "I beg your pardon?"

"For you to turn my feelings against me this way."

"What in the world are you talking about? My offer has nothing to do with your feelings. You said yourself you're looking to find a new direction. This seems like a win-win for all."

"Does it? Because from where I'm standing it seems to be a way for you to keep me nearby but still at arm's length."

He bolted up and reached her in two strides. "That's ridiculous."

She ignored his denial and jabbed a finger against his chest, trying desperately not to notice how hard and muscular he felt. "Is it? And what about Sonya in all of this?"

"What about her?"

"Has it once occurred to you that rather than another therapist or a new activity, Sonya might just need some time and attention? Specifically, your time and attention."

"What?"

"And instead of trying to provide that, you're trying to use me—no, you're trying to *buy* me to provide those things as a substitute."

Jordan's jaw clenched and his expression hardened. "Forget it, Jess. Forget I even mentioned it."

"Oh, no, you don't. Much too late for that. The cat's out of the bag already."

"Listen, I get it. I didn't mean to overstep. You're not ready to take any sort of step toward a career decision obviously. Not even for Sonya's sake."

He may as well have picked her up and thrown her into the pool.

"How dare you," she said, unable to keep the angry tremor from her voice. "You know very well that I grew to love that sweet little girl right around the same time I fell in love with you!"

She clapped a hand to her mouth before she could say any more. But it was too late. Jordan had heard enough. The loaded word now hung heavy in the air between them.

Suddenly, she felt utterly deflated, completely weary. Why hadn't she just left as soon as Sonya got out of the pool? Her heart would at least be in one piece right now, if somewhat wounded, if only she'd done just that. Instead, now it was completely in shatters. "What exactly is it that you want from me, Jordan? Can you just come out and say it?"

"Damn it, Jess. I didn't mean—"

He didn't get a chance to finish. For the second time that afternoon, Elise happened to interrupt them. She opened the screen door again and popped her head out.

"Jess, any interest in staying for dinner? We'd love to have you."

Jess didn't take her eyes off Jordan's face when she answered. "I can't. I'm sorry."

Jordan could only watch Jess as she stormed past him. By the time she reached the side of the house she was at a near jog. She couldn't wait to get away from him.

"Please tell Sonya I had to leave and that I said goodbye," she threw over her shoulder to Elise. The fury emanating off her could be felt even from this distance. What the hell had he done?

Elise came to stand next to him and they both watched her leave. "What did I miss?" she asked.

"Damned if I know."

"Any chance you would know if you'd been paying attention?"

Jordan pinched the bridge of his nose. "I'm not sure what that means but I had an idea the other day that I decided to share with her."

"What kind of idea?"

Jordan explained in general terms. He barely

had time to finish before Elise whirled on him. “You did what?”

“I don’t understand why my suggestion is so wrong.” The sound of Jess’s car door slamming echoed through the air from the driveway. “Why did it warrant that reaction?”

But Elise didn’t answer, simply rubbed her fingers over her forehead. “Oh, Jordan. What are we to do with you?”

Jordan was still wondering about the answer to Elise’s question as he walked back onto the patio later that evening. He was on his second glass of wine but the alcohol wasn’t doing much to dull the feeling of restlessness deep within his chest. Sonya was in bed for the night. Elise was apparently done dealing with him. She’d barely spoken during and after dinner. Then she’d retired to her cottage two hours ago.

Jess’s angry words resonated in his head. She’d said he had found a way to keep her at arm’s length while still close.

Was that really what he’d been trying to do when he’d made his offer? Even in some small way?

But that notion made no sense, regardless of

what Jess thought his motives were. He would have tried to explain if she hadn't stormed off the way she did. He'd simply seen how happy Sonya was to have Jess here. He'd seen the way Jess was genuinely invested in Sonya's progress, the genuine affection in her eyes as she applauded his sisters efforts just this afternoon as she swam.

And Jess seemed so uncertain about her own future path. He figured he could help her along. It all seemed to fall into place as far as he was concerned.

Jordan swallowed another swig of the aged cabernet and cursed out loud. If there was even a possibility that he'd somehow used Jess's affection for Sonya as any kind of leverage, even subconsciously, what did that say about him?

He didn't want to examine that question too closely.

And there was also something else she'd said that he was trying not to examine. In her fury, she'd blurted out that she'd fallen in love with him. But surely she had to be exaggerating the sense of attraction she was feeling. Nothing more than that, he was certain. She didn't know him well enough to be in love with him. Jess was confusing attraction and passion for love. He knew better. They may have been intimate in New York but their actions had been the result of an intense heat-of-the-moment passion where they'd both succumbed to desire.

He thought about calling her. To try and explain. Maybe he should even go over there to her apartment to do so face-to-face. That idea was nixed in an instant. He couldn't explain what he didn't have the words for. Plus, there was a high probability she would slam the door in his face.

No, it was better to just let the matter blow over. And to give her time to cool off. The next time he saw her, she'd be over the anger and perhaps then they could really talk.

He couldn't guess when that would be. With the community center shut down for days, what were the chances of randomly running into Jess even given the size of Martha's Vineyard? Maybe it was better that way. They both needed to cool off for a bit. But he couldn't stand the prospect of not seeing her smiling at him or hearing that melodic laugh of hers for days or maybe even weeks.

Jordan stood and started to pace, sloshing

some of the wine in the process. Such a waste but he could hardly bring himself to care. He didn't even know what he wanted anymore. What had happened to him since moving out here?

Wrong question. A more fitting one would be to ask what had happened to him since meeting *her*.

He'd always prided himself on knowing exactly what he wanted and how to go about getting it. Even after life had thrown him a curveball in the form of a tiny little girl who had no one else, he made sure he had a purpose. But then Sonya's accident had happened. Her hearing issues started immediately after. All his priorities shifted overnight. It didn't make any kind of difference how many times the experts told him the two events were unrelated. The injuries Sonya had suffered were unlikely to have caused damage to even one ear, let alone both. The doctors had all been unanimous. At the most, they all agreed, the trauma might have triggered a genetic predisposition to a hearing impairment.

On the surface that all made sense. But Jordan didn't care.

The accident had been his fault.

Jess had no idea how unworthy of her love he really was.

Jess sat in front of her laptop staring into the dark screen. As much as she needed to talk to someone right now, she felt selfish for what she was thinking of doing.

She moved her fingers over the keyboard to call up the contact option for the one person on earth who'd been there for her since they'd first met. Then she shut the laptop closed with a deep, resounding sigh. She couldn't do it. Kelly had enough to deal with, between managing a demanding toddler and another infant due any day. Any minute perhaps. Kelly was that far along. Jess couldn't bring herself to dump her own problems on her already overextended friend.

She'd just sit here and nurse her wounds on her own with a pint of Bimby's mocha chip. She'd stopped by for some on the way home from Jordan's.

She popped off the lid and reached for her spoon. But the ice cream could only do so much. She set it back down and lifted the laptop open once more. Would it really be so bad to video chat Kelly? After all, she should probably check on her anyway. Without giving herself a chance to back out, she hit the appropriate button. Kelly's smiling yet clearly tired face appeared on the screen a moment later.

"Hey, bff."

"Hey. Long time, no speak."

Kelly pointed to the screen. "Is that Bimby's? Lordy, I miss that place."

"I'll try to find a way to ship some to you."

Kelly patted her belly. "Baby and I would very much appreciate it if you started working on that immediately. What flavor have you got?"

"Mocha chip."

Kelly drew back. "Uh-oh. I distinctly recall you only got that particular one when you were upset or angry. Or both."

Here was reason number thirty thousand why Kelly was her best friend. The woman knew her so well, down to which flavors went with her mood.

Jess heard the wail of a small voice in the background.

"I don't want to keep you, Kelly. Your son sounds like he needs you."

"Well, it sounds like my dearest friend needs me, too. And my son happens to have another parent in there with him. So, fess up already. What's got you so upset?"

"You may find it all hard to believe."

Kelly gasped on the screen in front of her. "A man! Jessalyn Nadia Raffi, you've been holding out on me. You met someone?" she asked with an excited squeal. Then her eyes narrowed into a squint. "Wait. What did he do? Did he hurt you in any way? I'll have to fly down and throttle him."

Jess laughed out loud, the first genuine hint of amusement she'd felt since leaving Jordan's house this afternoon. "You don't do a lot of web surfing or TV watching, do you?"

Kelly actually snorted. "Are you kidding? If I have so much as a free minute, it's to catch up on some much-needed sleep. Same with David. He's really picked up a lot of the slack around here now that I'm too pregnant to move much. Why?"

"He's a good one, that David."

Kelly sighed. “Yes, I know. I’m lucky to have him.” True affection sounded in her voice.

“He’s lucky to have you.”

“I know that, too.” She leaned in closer to the monitor. “Hold on a minute. Are you saying I might have seen something about you if I’d been online recently?”

Jess gave a shake of her head. “Never mind, it’s not important.”

“Listen, bff, I want to know what’s going on with you. I miss you.”

Jess felt the sudden sting of tears. “I miss you, too.”

“Not to mention I’m in desperate need of some adult conversation that doesn’t revolve around toddler sleep patterns or Braxton-Hicks contractions.”

“Well, I was going to ask you about those at some point.”

Kelly shifted in her seat as if she couldn’t get comfortable. “Please don’t. Tell me what’s going on with you instead.”

Jess sucked in a deep breath and began to relay the whole series of events, starting with her spontaneous decision to draw the castle on the wall. By the time she finished, she’d dabbed at her eyes more than once and was feeling completely spent. The telling felt like a release, a catharsis of sort. Kelly had done exactly what she'd needed her to do—she'd simply listened in silence. The slightest noise she'd made had been when Jess got to the part about Jordan's offer. That was the part Jess had almost gotten too choked up to speak.

"Oh, Jess. You've really fallen for him, haven't you? Like head-over-heels fallen," Kelly said, concern and empathy etched in her voice from thousands of miles away.

Jess sniffled. "Is it that obvious?"

"I'm afraid so. I've never seen you so worked up over a man before. Not even that bore Gary."

Well, that certainly was an apt way to describe things. Every time she saw Jordan she came away from the encounter worked up in one way or another.

"There are clearly things he's not saying to you, honey. Things he hasn't even admitted to himself."

"To be fair, he never led me on, Kelly. In fact, he made sure I knew exactly where he stood."

Kelly responded with a sympathetic nod. "Give him points for being up-front, I guess."

Jess rubbed a shaky hand down her face. "If only he was being as direct with himself."

Her friend leaned farther into the screen. "I guess he needs time. To adjust and somehow find a way to forgive himself and also to figure out how to be the parent that his sister needs. So I need to ask you something."

"What's that?"

"Are you willing to wait for him? At least for a while. I mean, no one would suggest you wait forever."

Jess didn't answer out loud. But deep inside she knew. She'd known since that first day when she'd been covered in paint and dressed in farmer's overalls and Jordan had walked into the room startling her. When she'd first laid eyes on him.

"Your silence tells me a great deal," Kelly continued. "So just one more question."

"What's that?"

"Why haven't you told him so yet? That you're willing to wait for him?"

CHAPTER FIFTEEN

JESS WAS STILL thinking about her friend's question as she poured her third cup of coffee the next morning. After a restless night spent tossing and turning, she hadn't gotten any kind of real sleep. Since getting out of bed, she'd tried to take her mind off the events of yesterday by attempting about twelve different sketches. None of her ideas seemed to hold her interest for much longer than a few minutes before she tore off each sheet and crumpled it into a ball. Maybe she'd never want to draw another thing for the rest of her life. That possibility seemed quite feasible at this point.

Why haven't you told him so yet?

Kelly's words echoed through her mind. On the surface it seemed such a simple query. But could she do it? Could Jess open herself any further and risk exposing her heart to any more pain?

The answer came in the form of yet another

question: Would she ever forgive herself if she didn't take the chance?

Every moment she'd spent with Jordan was vividly ingrained in her memory. Everything that had happened between them in Manhattan would be forever etched in her brain.

Suddenly, Jess knew exactly what she wanted to create. She pulled the sketch pad back out and flipped it to a fresh page. Then she began to draw.

This was probably a mistake.

Jordan nearly turned away from Jess's door without knocking. The last time he'd given her a bouquet seemed like ages ago. In that instance she'd promptly informed him that he'd overdone it.

The bouquet he held today was much less extravagant. A simple bundle of pink roses. He probably should have had them delivered by the florist rather than showing up at her apartment himself. But he wanted to see her in person.

Without allowing any more thought, he rapped lightly on the door, which opened within moments. A very surprised Jess stood on the other side.

"Jordan?"

"Hey. Hope I'm not intruding."

She gave her head a small shake. "What are you doing here?" Her gaze dropped to the roses he held in his hand. "More flowers?"

"Apology roses this time. Just one solitary bouquet."

She stepped to the side and gestured with her arm. "Please, come in."

He handed her the roses as he passed by.

"They're lovely," she said and inhaled deeply of the floral scent. "I'll just put these in water."

When she returned a few moments later, Jordan was still debating exactly what he wanted to say and how he might say it.

They'd had such an easy camaraderie during the trip to New York City. They'd spent the night locked in each other's arms as close as two people can be. Yet, now here he was, at a loss for words.

"You're going to make Ray down at the nursery very happy and wealthy if you keep apologizing with flowers." She set the vase down on a wooden side table and came to stand before him.

"He mentioned the pink roses were very popular."

Jess merely nodded with a tight smile. Jordan resisted the urge to swear out loud. The conversation between them was so strained, so unnatural. He knew every inch of her body, but he didn't know how to talk to her.

He had to try. And he had to start with the very subject he'd been trying to avoid. Jordan cleared his throat.

"I've been thinking a lot about what you said. That Sonya needs my time and attention." He released a deep sigh, unsure exactly how to continue. "It occurs to me that I can't really provide her with those things until I face what happened."

He wasn't surprised when she guessed immediately what he was referring to. "Jordan, you have to forgive yourself. Sonya's hearing loss is not your fault."

He couldn't help himself. He had to touch her. Putting his hands on her waist he pulled her closer, rested his forehead against hers. "I might need some help with that."

He felt her exhale in his arms. The scent of her surrounded him, her warmth as comforting as a lazy summer morning. "What kind of help?" she asked.

Jordan grasped for just the right words. Pulling back slightly, he focused on those bright hazel eyes he'd grown so fond of. "I've realized I need you by my side as I come to terms with it all."

"You have?" she asked on a stutter.

"Without a doubt. Don't you see, Jess?"

She sucked in her bottom lip and he almost lost focus. "See what?"

"You're the reason I want to try."

Shock widened her eyes. "I am?"

"Yes. I want you to be there to see that I can handle raising a little girl. That I have what it takes to be a strong figure in her life. I'll never be her father, but I can be the parental figure she needs. Until you came along, I wasn't sure I was up to the challenge. I'd convinced myself that I'd already failed beyond redemption."

She immediately countered that statement with a vehement shake of her head, her thick, wavy hair bouncing around her shoulders. "You haven't. Not in the least."

There it was. The unwavering faith she had in him. All these weeks she'd been showing him that faith in so many different ways, both big and small. He'd just been too blind to see it until it was almost too late.

"But I don't think I can do any of it without you," he admitted. "I know it's a lot to ask."

She surprised him by planting a full, hard kiss on his lips. He immediately reacted by pulling her even closer. A hairsbreadth separated them.

"Oh, Jordan. I'm so glad that you're asking it of me."

He dropped a kiss to the top of her head. "Who else would I ask it of? But the woman I seem to have fallen in love with."

Jess wanted to stop time, to somehow make this moment last for all eternity. She settled deeper into Jordan's embrace. If it was up to her, she'd ask that he never let go.

His words from a moment ago echoed through her head. He wanted her by his side as he navigated the challenges of parenthood. Only her.

He'd fallen in love with her.

And she'd been falling for him since the day she'd thrown a wet paintbrush at his silk white shirt.

They stood that way for several minutes, the analog clock on the wall behind them loudly ticking away the time. Finally, the pinging sound of an incoming text on his phone broke the silence. Jordan looked at the screen and a small chuckle escaped his lips.

"What is it?"

"A reminder from my little sister."

"About?"

"I promised her I'd make a stop at Bimby's for some ice cream on the way home. Guess I better not keep her waiting." Before he got far, his gaze suddenly dropped to the sketch pad that had been sitting on the coffee table the whole time. Jess had forgotten all about where she'd dropped it upon discovering Jordan at her door.

Jordan picked it up and studied it. "Is that…?"

"It's the photograph from your apartment," Jess admitted with no small amount of apprehension. There was a chance Jordan wouldn't appreciate what she'd drawn. He might even feel resentful. Well, there was no turning back now.

"I sketched it for you. To give you when the time was right." Only she'd foolishly left it lying around so now the decision was out of her hands.

He rubbed a finger down along the paper as if outlining the image. "I don't know what to say."

"Please know that I wasn't invading your privacy that day. I was just looking for something to sketch with and I came across the photograph."

He didn't look up from the pad for several moments, and the blood turned cold in her veins. If he was upset with her for drawing it, her heart might shatter in her chest.

"I'm glad you did," he finally said.

Jess blew out the breath she'd been holding in relief. "You are?"

"Yes. But what compelled you to do this?"

There was no real good way to explain. She took a deep breath, grasping for the right words. "I felt like I knew you better once I saw that photograph. Does that make any sense?"

The way his eyes searched her face gave her the answer to that question. She tried again. "That photo manages to capture who you were as a boy. Your hopes for the future are almost written right there in the way you look at the camera. But when I look at it closely, I can also see the man that boy becomes. With all his strengths and all his weaknesses. It's all there, in the set of your features, the expression on your face, the look in your eyes. I saw the man I was falling in love with when I found the photo that day."

His response was another lingering kiss that set her skin on fire. "That's amazing," he whispered against her lips afterward.

It took a moment for her to find her voice. "I don't know about that. It's just what I see. I had to re-create it on paper."

"You're pretty amazing yourself, Jess."

She didn't allow herself to dwell on the compliment. She didn't feel amazing. Some sketches simply came easier than others. "It's just a simple pencil sketching."

"I mean more than your artistic talent. I mean the way you paint elaborate castles on walls for children you haven't even met yet. The way you delight in watching a theater production but your immediate thought is that you want your young students to be able to watch it also. The way you take time out of your weekend to help your boss with her budget woes. Not to mention the way you seem to have found your way into my heart when it was the last thing I was expecting."

Jess felt the sting of joyful tears behind her eyes. He really did see all that in her. The knowledge served to finally break the guarded walls she'd built around her heart all these years.

"The sketch is yours if you want it," she offered once she found her voice.

He stepped closer to her and cupped her chin in his palm, then lifted her face to his. "I want it."

Jess willed her knees to keep from buckling underneath her.

"And I want this," he added, then placed another kiss on her lips. This time it was the faintest brush of contact. It was just enough to take her breath away.

EPILOGUE

THE AIR WAS definitely chillier than the last time they'd been up here. But Jess didn't mind the cold. She was right where she wanted to be at this moment—atop Jordan's building once more, watching the breathtaking New York skyline. The weather wasn't the only thing that was different since that fateful summer night he'd first brought her up here. Everything had changed. In ways she could have only dreamed of.

"Cold?" Jordan asked behind her. He held her tight against him, her back to his chest as they admired the view.

"Maybe just a little," she admitted, snuggling just a bit tighter against his length.

"I'll just have to see what I can do about that," he teased, trailing his lips softly down the side of her neck. His kisses immediately had the desired effect. Her blood heated in her veins.

"That definitely warmed me up, Mr. Paydan."

"But you're still shivering. I guess I better get started, then." He spoke against her ear, his breath warm against her cheek.

"Started?"

"I brought you up here for a reason." Jess felt him reach inside his pocket. She shifted to turn and face him.

"More than just to admire the beautiful view?"

"Yes, there's more." He handed her a square cardboard box with delicate gold trim decorating each corner. "I also wanted to give you this." Jess uncovered the lid to find a playbill inside.

"Are we going to see another show?"

He nodded. "Not just us."

What was he up to? "I don't understand."

"I secured a whole section of seats. For the children and their parents. Whoever wants to attend. You said that day that you wished your students were there to watch the matinee with us."

He'd remembered that. And all these months later he was giving her that wish. How had she possibly gotten so lucky to have found this man? "Jordan, this is so sweet of you, so thoughtful. I don't know what to say. Aside from thank you." Though it seemed hardly adequate. The thought that had gone into his gesture had tears stinging her eyes.

"Consider it an engagement present."

Jess's breath caught. Had she just heard him correctly? Between the noise of the wind gusting around them and the sudden pounding of her pulse, it was hard to be sure. Maybe her mind was playing tricks on her, having her imagine that she was hearing things she would be elated to hear.

But then Jordan took a knee and reached for her hand. In his palm, he held another box—this one small, velvet and black. He flipped the cover open to reveal a square-cut stone that glimmered like the bright city lights in the distance.

"Jordan?" She barely managed to get his name out. Emotion flooded from her chest down to her very toes.

"Jessalyn Nadia Raffi, would you do me the honor of attending this show as my future wife?"

He'd barely gotten the last word out before she answered him. "Yes!"

And then her voice simply failed her. Her very equilibrium seemed to have fled. She could barely remain upright as time seemed to stop. Jordan took the ring out of the satin cushion and slipped it on her trembling finger. Jess felt as if she was watching a dream play out in the middle of the night.

Then he stood and took her lips with his own. And she knew all her dreams had just come true.

* * * * *